THE CONDOR CONSPIRACY

Charlotte Yarborough

When old John Chilton – veteran reporter, in Panama working on the biggest story of his life – was found dead, his beautiful niece Jimmie set out to find the killer.

With the help of Roberto Villalba, scion of a powerful Panamanian family, she pieced together the puzzle of the Condor, a secret nationalist alliance bent on the destruction of the state.

On the eve of a crucial treaty signing, with the fate of the country in jeopardy, Jimmie and Roberto came face to face with members of the sinister conspiracy and risked their lives in a gamble that could plunge a continent into war!

THE CONDOR CONSPIRACY

CHARLOTTE YARBOROUGH

Curley Publishing, Inc.
South Yarmouth, Ma.

Library of Congress Cataloging-in-Publication Data

Yarborough, Charlotte.
  The condor conspiracy / Charlotte Yarborough.
    p. cm.
  1. Large type books. I. Title.
[PS3575.A68C6 1989]
813'.54—dc19
ISBN 1–55504–916–8 (lg. print)   89–1286
ISBN 1–55504–917–6 (pbk. : lg. print)   CIP

Published in Large Print by arrangement with Dorchester Publishers, Inc. in the United States, Canada, the U.K. and British Commonwealth.

Distributed in Great Britain, Ireland and the Commonwealth by CHIVERS LIBRARY SERVICES LIMITED, Bath BA1 3HB, England.

Printed in Great Britain

To R

1
THE YELLOW HOUSE

The trade winds stirred the wooden slatted blinds; afternoon light over the marina stained the room's white walls pale gold, flecked an obsidian jaguar on the desk.

Roberto groped for a banana among the papers and books, and absently laid it on top of a blue-scrolled pottery jar made a thousand years ago by Coclé Indians.

The desk, about half the age of the jar, of dark carved walnut, had been brought to Panama from Spain in the sixteenth century by his ancestors.

Roberto ate the banana and looked at the shadow-reproduction of the jaguar on the white wall. Good work, he thought, wishing he had drawn it.

The blinds swayed so far into the room that he could see the purple flowers growing on the upper patio.

"Beguilements," he thought. At night the ilangilang would perfume both the lower and upper patio of the yellow house.

He looked at his watch. Eduardo's class was at five o'clock.

The paper that Roberto was reading was one of the pile of themes written by his half-brother Eduardo's students. Eduardo Villalba was professor of literature at the Universidad Nacional. He was also the youngest member of the Panamanian Assembly and a junior partner in a law firm. His professional life was a series of acrobatics which would have been impossible to sustain without heavy reliance on Roberto's help. Moreover, Eduardo's social life was energetic; he needed time for tennis; and he had a boat, the forty-five foot *Isla Amarilla*, of which he was prouder, Roberto thought, than of inherited treasures, the yellow house, or his family itself.

Eduardo had used his small legacy from their father and had borrowed most of Roberto's to buy the *Isla*. Sometimes he chartered it so that during its absences Roberto was relieved of the painting and repair work for which, unfortunately, he had the talent.

Roberto's profusion of interests and his studies, as a senior at the University, seemed irrelevant to Eduardo because his own pursuits were more spectacular than his brother's.

2

Their aunt, Teresa, who lived with them, thought Eduardo's assumptions reasonable and added her own demands upon Roberto's time. The household was disorganized and frequently in crisis over money. These problems, Roberto thought, welded the family together, making his aunt and Eduardo less conscious of his own half-alienness: his mother had been North American. Teresa, their father's sister, naturally felt closer to Eduardo, the older and wholly Panamanian nephew. Roberto recognized the cleavage but did not resent it; he found both Teresa and Eduardo interesting, even fascinating, often wished he were more like them, and if he was too clear-minded not to realize that he was imposed upon, was too fond of them to object. The trouble was that he never got anything really finished. There were the notes for his paper on Cervantes's *Novelas*, for a course; there was a half-finished book review for the newspaper Ahora – San Martin, the editor and owner, would pay him promptly for that if he could ever get it done; there were books he had to read for a history course; there was a Portuguese grammar (he wanted to learn the language because he had met a pleasant girl at a party at the Brazilian Embassy); and most important, there were

3

books to read and an article to write about the Coclé culture. He loved the sound of the name Coclé; loved everything he knew about the Indians whose name it had been centuries ago; loved the land running from mountains to the Pacific where they had built their temples and their statues. Some of that land he and Eduardo owned – a part of the site of recent digs by an expedition. Roberto went to the site whenever he could and dug with rapture, but he had been too busy to go there for over a year.

No use thinking about Coclé or Cervantes. He had to read the rest of the themes. This one, which he had just finished, was laid aside because he would have to tell Eduardo about it. Part of his duty as reader was to keep Eduardo informed about students who were related to important persons, such as the sons or daughters of politicians or ambassadors. The name signed to this theme was North American. How had he missed it before? Eduardo never assigned written work; it had been Roberto himself, substituting for Eduardo, who had given the assignment. And since Eduardo had lost his roll book early in the term, the attendance had not been taken. Mid-March, Roberto thought, and called, "Eduardo!"

Eduardo came into the room, clinking ice

4

cubes in a glass of rum punch. He looked sleekly exuberant after exercise, but Roberto recognized the peculiar gaiety which covered tension or worry. Eduardo crossed the room, his tennis shoes sucking on the buff and white tiles, and threw his arm across Roberto's shoulders.

"Finished, hombré?"

"Nearly."

"What would I do without you?"

Roberto shrugged.

"You know I am grateful," Eduardo said.

"You're going to meet your class this evening?" Roberto asked hopefully.

"Impossible."

"But you missed the class last week. Please go tonight."

"The people who are chartering the *Isla* are up the coast near here. I want to look in on them. To see that everything is all right."

"But the class starts at five – go there first, can't you?"

"Oh, I suppose so. You are right, *chico*. I might go for the hour, but first I need to get some money." He glanced toward the open door to the patio where light had cooled to an agate green, then looked at his brother.

"*Chico*, you look appalling. Have you a mirror?"

5

He leaned forward and twisted the lock of hair that fell over Roberto's forehead. "Your hair needs trimming, and wearing those frightful white canvas trousers – that old blue shirt – those tattered huaraches – oh, *chico*, must you always wear your glasses?"

"Only if I want to see anything," Roberto said dryly. "As for the haircut –"

"Don't say what I think you will say – oh no – it isn't – Roberto, you mean you have no money either?"

"How did you guess?"

"But – I have none – I suppose *tia Teresa* is out?"

"Yes."

"But I thought you would be paid for your review – the newspaper?"

"I haven't had time to finish it."

Eduardo tapped his brother's shoulder.

"Never mind. I will do something. Find some – borrow a little – but then I cannot meet that class. Look, *chico*, get the barber to cut your hair – he will let you pay later. Put on something else – meet my class?"

Roberto shuffled the themes together, saying nothing.

"It is not our fault, entirely," his brother said. "The payment from the coffee *finca* is held up – there is that unfortunate change in the purchasing system – by the Canal

6

Zone – they will take the coffee beans – it's just a delay while they reorganize their accounting system. If we can get through tonight –"

"Eduardo. I don't want to go into Panama City tonight. I want to drive out to Coclé."

"Why?"

"I like it. I haven't been there for almost a year. I like the smell of the old vanished Indians. And I want to dig."

Eduardo gripped the edge of the desk with long slim hands.

"Roberto, if I had one request in all time to make of you, it would be that you do *not* dig at Coclé."

"Why?"

"It is not good for you, *chico* – to grub in the past. To let your hair grow ragged and dig for old broken pottery – no, please, promise me you will not go out to Coclé."

"Like hell I'll promise!" Roberto answered in English. He told himself that Eduardo could make himself look stricken; it was an act; but still –

"Eduardo, you don't mean it?"

"I mean it. I beg you to give up this useless digging. Or at least wait until I can go with you."

"Why should you go with me?"

"Because you are too much alone."

7

Roberto laughed.

"You aren't here very much to keep me from being alone."

"I know," Eduardo said contritely. "But it will be different, and I will make a bargain with you. I will meet my classes every day. Or at least once a week without fail. If you will not dig at Coclé."

This bargain, Roberto thought, was almost worth making. He worried about those classes of his brother's. Ironical, though, that the promise to meet them should be handed to him at a bribe.

"All right. I'll accept. Beginning –"

"Well, tonight," Eduardo said unhappily.

"Relax. I'll take over tonight. Beginning tomorrow."

"You are a good boy, and I will trim your hair."

"Dios! *You* will?"

His brother brought scissors and comb and razor and started the trimming with such assurance that Roberto's misgivings subsided.

"Not bad, not bad at all."

"Wait until I finish. You will see the world has lost a fine barber, *chico.*"

They both laughed and said at the same moment, "Toto."

8

The sharing of the reminiscence revived the comradeship of earlier and unworried days.

"Of course," Eduardo said, "a sheep dog offers limitless possibilities to a small boy with scissors. But what were you trying to do to Toto?"

"Two things," Roberto said. "I wanted to see whether he would unravel. And I wanted to give him a beard, like the ones in the portraits of our ancestors."

"I stopped you just in time. There, *hermanito,* how do you like your hair?"

"Admirable," Roberto said, wishing he could prolong the performance, wishing they could return, if only for an hour, to that past. What hour would he choose? Perhaps one of those times in the library, when Eduardo and he had read old diaries and records kept by their forebears.

Despite the eight years' difference in age, Roberto thought he and Eduardo had with remarkable congeniality shared the sixteenth century and much else. Lately, however, their communication had thinned. For a few minutes during the haircutting and the reminiscence about Toto, they had tapped an underlying comradeship, but only for those few minutes.

"I hope you have something presentable to wear," Eduardo said.

"Yes. The old white linen suit. Ready to fall apart but pure. By the way, there's a VIP relative in your class. Here's his paper. Chilton. Jimmie Chilton."

Eduardo frowned at the signature.

"Well, VIP or not?" Roberto said. "Our neighbor, the journalist, in the apartment building next door."

"Oh, VIP, yes," Eduardo said slowly. "The old man's famous. A walking threat because he knows so much. He has lived here so long that people forget he is a North American. I have heard it said that his papers hold enough dynamite to explode three governments."

"He has never blasted a government," Roberto said. "Well – maybe once. I wouldn't remember. But I think he is –" Roberto lapsed into English – "quite a guy. And if you have his nephew or something in your class, – you ought to know."

"Frankly, *chico*, I don't know what I've got in that class. You know them better than I. Do you remember a North American boy?"

"I get stage fright," Roberto said. "I don't notice faces. You know I can't enchant them

10

the way you do. I have to work with them. Or try to."

"Well, never give written assignments. By the way, what did this boy write about?"

"He wrote about this house."

"What did you tell them to write about, misguided child?"

"About something in Panama they valued."

Eduardo laughed. "Oh, no! That is too good – Chilton's nephew – writing about our house! What did he say?"

"Rather poetic," Roberto said. "Description. Managed to use a good phrase – ancient beauty. Used subjunctives pretty well. If you kept a roll book and called the roll –"

"Yes, my conscience, you're right. Ah, well, Roberto, you can save the white linen suit. I will meet this class."

Roberto shrugged. Unpredictable brother I have, he thought.

Roberto finished reading the themes in time to give them to Eduardo; then completed the book review, wondering, as he put the pages into an envelope, whether he had gone too far, even for his editor's liberality, in criticizing the book as a florid and bombastic support of privilege and the status quo of Panama's elite, as opposed to the efforts of men in the professions and in

11

government who were trying to bridge the gap between power and poverty.

He took a shower and put on the white suit, cautiously; its hours were numbered.

On his way out, he returned the scissors and comb and razor that Eduardo had left on the desk. Eduardo's room, as usual, surprised him by its neatness. He had not gone into it lately; for a long time there had been none of the talks with which they had used to end the day, casual talks over cups of chocolate; but in the past, Eduardo's engagements had not kept him out for most, if not all, the night. And there had been more to talk about, leisurely, without the prod of their anxiety about money as the costs of living went up.

Only the desk showed disorder, minor compared with the clutter of Roberto's. He noticed sheets of paper covered with his brother's handwriting; two books whose leather bindings were crumbling; an ornament from a girl's hair; and a map of the state of Coclé. My map, Roberto thought, recognizing notes he made on the margin, a surveyor's map, on which the Villalba land was outlined in red. He hadn't missed it.

His aunt Teresa's voice called, "Eduardo," and she came through the open doorway. "Oh, you, *chico*. Where is your brother?"

12

The black dress, Roberto thought, was airy enough to look cool. Her shimmering black hair, rolled high, made her seem taller than her five feet five inches – that, or the high-heeled black slippers. The somber black-outlined eyes were theatrical in the pallor of her face. No wonder, he thought, that she was often taken for Eduardo's sister. She was thirty-nine but looked twenty-five.

"Eduardo has gone to the University. He has a class."

"But what are you doing here, *chico?*"

"Returning some things of his. And I notice he has my map of Coclé. I didn't think he had ever been interested in our holdings there."

"Perhaps he thinks of selling some of the land." She sighed. "So tiresome always to need money. It need not have happened – if your father had not been so – fastidious."

"Fastidious or scrupulous?" Roberto asked.

She shrugged. "Whatever you wish. But he learned about the road that was to be built. He could have bought land and later sold it for three times what he paid. Many people use such information. Well, I have an engagement. I was going to ask Eduardo to drive me but will now have to telephone for a taxi."

13

"I can drive you," Roberto offered.

"No, *chico,* not in your car, which always looks unhappy and not clean. However – could you lend me five *balboas?*"

"I am sorry. I can't. Not now. I am going to deliver a book review to the newspaper."

Teresa frowned.

"Those reviews. Roberto, someone told me your reviews are displeasing to certain important people. And so is the newspaper you write for."

"Who objects? The Condor – if there is a Condor?" he laughed.

"That is not for us to discuss. Please remember, however, that your brother has a political career ahead of him, and you are not helping him. I suggest that you behave with some maturity, no?"

The scorn in her voice made Roberto conscious of his separation from the two other members of his family.

2
XIMENA

Eduardo made an entrance casual enough to show his feeling of sympathy for the twenty some students awaiting him, yet lofty enough to mark the intricacies of his intellectual and social experience.

Having glanced through the papers on his way to the class, he could deliver some general comments. Easy enough, then, to branch into a talk about the elements of literature, of Spanish literature, of literature in the Western Hemisphere – and on to a name or two – Rubén Dario, Cortázar, Valle Inclán, Unamuno, Carlos Fuentes – the smooth young faces, dark and fair, in front of him looked receptive – the period was ending.

"Well then," Eduardo said, "Go to the library. Read from books by the men I have named. Be ready to tell me how you find them. What meaning the thoughts of these men have for you. And will señor Chilton please remain a moment?"

The student who stayed after the others

had gone was a girl. Approaching the desk with composure and diffidence, she looked at Eduardo through violet-blue eyes and said in Spanish, "I wonder if you want to see me, señor. I am Jimmie Chilton."

"*You* are Jimmie Chilton?" Then, yes, it is you whom I wish to see. But you are señorita Chilton. Perhaps you have a brother?"

"No. Jimmie is short for Ximena."

"You are not Panamanian"

"North American. I had a Spanish great-grandmother."

How did I not notice this girl before, Eduardo wondered, this girl, so quiet, yet with such a brightness filtering through – the fair skin, the wash of tan – the hair that was neither dark nor light, a kind of golden chestnut? That dress, silver-gray cotton with a tone of green, the jade bracelet, the shaping of the hair, with the artless lock looping across the forehead – these details bore out impression of understatement, of freshness, and of an underlying sureness.

The most difficult age, he thought; for how could one know what pleasures to suggest, what stories to tell, when either element – the freshness or the competence – might predominate?

"It is a beautiful name out of the past.

16

Ximena. The beloved of El Cid." He spoke, not with the languid manner he would have used for an older woman but with a briskness compatible with her possible idea of a young professor.

She shifted the books she was carrying. A blue ballpoint pen fell from a pocket. Eduardo picked it up and took the books from her.

"You remind me of my brother," he said. "He always goes about carrying books. More than he will ever need."

Without the armload of books, she seemed a little bereft. "Did you want to see me about something?"

"For one thing, I wanted to ask whether you are perhaps a niece of señor John Chilton?"

"Yes. He is my great-uncle."

"You live with him – in the apartment over the marina?"

"No, I live with my sister and her husband in the Canal Zone. Do you know my uncle?"

"Everyone knows – or knows of – señor Chilton – of his writings – his journalistic work – his scholarship. He has lived here so long that we think of him as a Panamanian. But señorita, perhaps you would have time for a cup of coffee with me? I would

17

like to talk a little about your theme."

"Wasn't it satisfactory?"

"Claro que si," Eduardo assured her. "You will have coffee?"

"Well – yes, thank you."

They went down a stairway, into a passage open along the left to the broad sweep of emerald jungle and mountains that the University overlooked. The sea of treetops and the mountain slopes were scrolled with blue shadows.

"Beautiful, isn't it, señor?"

"The beauty is why I teach here," Eduardo said as they went into the coffee shop.

He led her among groups of chattering students, among textbooks piled on the floor, to a table. When a waiter had brought coffee, Eduardo said, "It is evident that you have a feeling for Panama. Your description of the yellow house had merit. By the way, do you know whose home it is?"

"No. I have seen the house from my uncle's apartment, and spoken of it, but he did not tell me who lived there."

"It is my home," Eduardo said.

"Yours? But how fortunate you are to live there!"

"It has been my family's home for many years. Our aunt lives with us. Perhaps some

18

day, you and your uncle will come to have tea with us, señorita?"

"I would like to," Jimmie said. "And maybe I could see some of the pottery made by the Coclé Indians. Your brother mentioned it one time when he was taking your place."

How like Roberto, Eduardo thought – to weave his own interests into my classroom.

"My brother assists me," he said, without enthusiasm.

At that moment, Roberto was entering the coffeeshop, looking over the tables. He saw Eduardo exerting his charm on an extremely pretty girl, who was undoubtedly captivated. He never misses, Roberto thought. Something about the girl was familiar – a student? Certainly he would have remembered her if he had seen her clearly before now.

He crossed the room and said, "Pardon me, Eduardo."

"Roberto, sit down, hombre. You must meet señorita Jimmie Chilton."

Roberto bowed but did not take the offered chair.

"We were discussing the señorita's theme. Do you know, Roberto – she wrote about the house in which we live?"

"How interesting," Roberto said. "I am

sorry to interrupt, but a telephone message came for you."

"I must leave," Jimmie said, rising.

"May I drive you home?" Eduardo asked.

"Thank you, but my car is here."

"Well, Roberto – the message?" Eduardo said, when she had gone.

"A girl's voice said that she had waited for you but could wait no longer."

Eduardo frowned.

"So señor Chilton's nephew became a niece," Roberto said as they walked toward the parking lot.

"I suggested that she and her uncle have tea at our house some afternoon."

"Do you think they will?"

"Probably not. But I wouldn't mind having a – what is your North American expression – pipeline? – into Chilton's current activities."

3
DINNER OVER THE MARINA

Around seven-thirty when John Chilton heard his West Indian housekeeper Victoria answer the doorbell, he took a manuscript page from his typewriter, placed the sheet with others in a desk drawer, and went into the living room to meet his niece.

"How cool here, like always," Jimmie said, leaving her books on a hall table and making for the terrace. In the marina below them, the tide was righting boats at their moorings. The water was rainbow-stained from lights along the shore's arc, and a moon of mid-growth had risen above the Pacific.

Victoria brought Scotch and soda for Chilton and sherry for Jimmie.

"Long day at the University?"

"Thursday's the day I have a five o'clock. Works out fine for coming here for dinner. But it's fine to be here any day."

A short distance to the right of her uncle's apartment building, the yellow house showed a light on the lower patio among the purple and white flowers.

"So that is where my professor lives," she said. "You didn't tell me."

"How's the course?"

"Good, but he doesn't usually meet it. His brother Roberto comes instead. Today, though, Eduardo was on deck. Seemed to like my paper – took me out for coffee."

"What do you think of him?"

"Rather dashing. Talks well but hops from one thing to another. He didn't seem to have any plan. I couldn't take notes. Roberto is better organized."

She giggled. Unseemly sound, her uncle thought, hoping she would outgrow the habit of making it.

"Well? What?"

"Eduardo said something ridiculous. That he taught at the University because the view was beautiful. I ask you!"

"Most unlikely," her uncle said. "I doubt whether a Villalba has ever been motivated by a sense of beauty. Not that the family hasn't accumulated admirable trappings. Spanish, Morisco. I've never been inside that house of theirs, but people who have tell me that it's like a museum – suits of armor – paintings – at least two by Velasquez. A gold dinner service. A library loaded with old leather-bound books. Unless the modern incompetents have sold their treasures. I've met Eduardo and the aunt, but I don't know Roberto. Does he take you out for coffee?"

"No. I think he's nearsighted."

"A modest statement if I ever heard one."

"Oh, I just meant I didn't think he knew me."

Her uncle produced the antique sound spelled hmph; he was the only person she knew who could have made it sound modern.

"Bring along your sherry," he said. "Vicky is signalling."

"Eduardo," Jimmie said as Victoria served them at the table near the living room windows, "wants you and me to have tea with them. Can we?"

"No."

"Why not?"

Her uncle cut a piece of steak and looked at it thoughtfully before eating it.

"I hope it's not tough, Mr. Chilton," Vicky said. "It's Panamanian beef. I couldn't get any from the States."

"It's good." To Jimmie he said, "The Villalbas are a very old family. Their lands here were granted by Charles V."

"No," Jimmie said. "That would make Eduardo almost four hundred years old."

"In some ways he is. Limelight family. An

23

ancestor got into trouble with Philip II because he was overzealous – he was captain of a ship in the Armada and not patient about following orders. Another ancestor plotted against Pizarro and was executed."

"Don't you ever have tea with people whose ancestors got into trouble?"

Her uncle chuckled. "I'm not fond of tea."

"Eduardo thinks you're quite a guy."

"I am overwhelmed."

Jimmie threw a strawberry at him.

"Careful. Those are imported from the States. Seriously, Jimmie, I think maybe you'd do better making more friends in the Canal Zone."

"Who's talking! How many times do you go over into the Zone? And that reminds me – Isabel and Glenn want you to come to a cocktail party on April 16. Please, will you?"

"I'll think about it. Any other persons coming from this side?"

"No. The Governor and his wife, the Chief of Personnel, some faculty members from the Zone College, and of course the new man, Clay Austin, an assistant to the Governor – he works under Glenn. Seems to throw all the women for a loop."

"But not you?"

"Not me." Jimmie laughed. "He uses funny words, like *whilst*. How could you loop for a man that said *whilst?* Reminds me of albeit – I used to think it was a misprint for *Albert.*"

"Albeit the Prince Consort." Her uncle tried it out.

"Who was he?"

"Where's your English history, miserable girl?"

"Dim."

"Have you perhaps heard of Queen Victoria?"

"Oh, her. Albert was her husband?"

"He was. And maybe you'd better take a course in English History."

"Oh hell," Jimmie said. "I've enough problems – if I fail chemistry, will you disown me? I can manage world lit and Spanish history all right, but my Spanish isn't up to chemistry."

"You're doing well enough even if you have to repeat chemistry. I'll find you a tutor if you want one."

"Mr. Chilton," Vicky said, serving dessert, "the little cat in the apartment over us climbed down the vines into our terrace and broke my plant with the blue flowers."

"I'll get you a new plant."

"I'd rather have a little cat."

25

"I'll think about that," Chilton said.

"Uncle John," Jimmie said. "How would you like to have a boarder for a while? Me. There's the maid's room – Vicky always goes home at night."

If her uncle had a fault – and she would not have admitted that he had one – it was that he did not answer questions directly. Now he asked, "Aren't you happy living with your sister?"

"Oh, Isabel and Glenn are easy to live with, and I get on all right with Tom – don't know why, though, because he's a weird kid. But I get tired of the way they apologize for me. For going to the University here. 'Trying it out,' they say, as if I were slumming. They seem to envy people in the Zone with children coming from the States for holidays from schools and colleges. Prestige items. So – how about it, my favorite relative? Take me as a lodger?"

Chilton went into his study and returned with a cigar, from which he took off a wrapper slowly.

Jimmie said diffidently and not hopefully, "Besides, if I lived here for a while, you could show me the Southern Cross. I'm never here late enough to see it. And I've lived down here for almost two years and not seen it."

26

"Can't you see it in the Canal Zone?"

At least, she thought, he had spoken.

When he had bared the cigar, he stood looking critically at it.

"I don't think it's a good idea, Jimmie," he said.

She looked at him sadly.

"Come along," he said, laying his hand on her shoulder. "We'll have coffee on the terrace. I'll offer you stars with your coffee, even if they aren't the Southern Cross."

Victoria brought them coffee.

"Well," Jimmie said, "any stars go well with coffee."

Chilton lighted his cigar.

"Understand this," he said. "I'm pleased – let's say flattered – that you want to stay here." He did not say how much he wanted her to come. "But my work makes enemies. Some of them aren't gentle. Now that the Canal Treaty controversy has heated up, I'm adding to my enemy list."

"I understand how you'd be making enemies in the States by supporting the Treaties, but here in Panama – aren't the people in favor of them?"

Her uncle did not answer immediately. Jimmie heard the tide in the marina wash against the retaining wall at the base of the apartment building. From the vines at the

27

outer side of the terrace a small wraith leaped to the floor and in the light from the doorway showed itself briefly as a slender cat before it darted into the living room, where Victoria could be heard offering it a cat delicacy.

"I'll have to let her have a kitten," Chilton said. "I can recognize the start of a campaign."

"Yes," Jimmie said. "But back to Panama?"

Chilton arced a cigar ash over the railing.

"A country sharply divided between the affluent and the impoverished is unstable. The instability may increase as a middle class develops. Here the middle class isn't strong enough to act as a buffer. And there are factions ready to take advantage of any opportunities to bring about a *coup détat*. They will work against peaceful settlements of long-time frictions like the friction with the United States and the more immediate resentment of the Canal Zone. And we have here – I say *we* because I've lived here so long – been fond of the country – we have a faceless force working against the elected members of the government and the actual head of state. Have you heard of the Condor?"

"Yes. Students at the University talk about the Condor. When somebody gets carried away – rightist or leftist – somebody else says, 'Shut up or I'll tell the Condor.' I've thought it was crazy – how could the Condor work both ways? Or is there really a Condor anyway?"

"The Condor," her uncle said, "is probably a group. Small. A virus. I'm investigating. I believe the Condor, whatever it is, is aiming to use any means to seize power."

"Do you know who the man or the group are?"

"I think so but couldn't prove anything. Not yet."

"You think the Condor – or Condors – are working against the Treaties?"

"Yes. To prolong instability. To create a crisis, in which they could seize power."

"It sounds complicated. And scary," Jimmie said. "You write about all this. People call you an investigative reporter."

"I think that's a poor term. A good reporter *is* investigative. It took me a long time to produce my books on Latin American affairs. I have masses of files and papers and dossiers and uncompleted case histories – some of them ready to go into articles or books when I can secure verifications."

Victoria came to refill the coffee cups. She

was a tall, slim, but strongly built Negro, light-skinned, with severe features that suggested some Indian ancestry, but with considerable warmth in her face when she smiled. She had worked for Chilton for eleven years. Jimmie was fond of her, and liked the nieces and nephews and their families with whom Victoria comfortably lived in two large adjoining apartments in *Avenida Central.* Years ago, Jimmie knew that Victoria's husband had been killed by a bull at a ranch outside the city, where he had been working.

Now, bearing the coffeepot, Victoria wore the neighboring cat over her left shoulder, tail down across her throat.

"You can have a cat, Vicky," Chilton said. "Can you find one or must I?"

"I know the cat I want, Mr. Chilton. My niece's cat had kittens a week ago."

"Cleverly staged," Chilton said. "Do I have to nursemaid the cat at night?"

"Oh, no, Mr. Chilton. I take him home when my nephew comes for me. No trouble for you."

"A jewel. A darling," Jimmie said when Victoria had left them.

"Stalwart," her uncle said. "One night Victoria was here late alone, making something for me over the weekend, when

30

somebody broke into the apartment. I'm telling you this so that you'll know what we're up against. The man was armed but Victoria beat him off with an iron skillet. Apologized later because a chicken concoction spattered over a rug. Over the intruder, too, I imagine."

"What do you think he wanted?"

"Probably papers – manuscript. Maybe sent by the Condor, who're probably skittish about what I've gathered."

"Did you have the locks changed?" Jimmie asked.

"Oh, yes. Better locks, and bolts added. I don't keep much of my material here. Only what I'm working on. Most of my papers are in a bank vault. My lawyer García and I have access to them. Nobody else. By the way, how is Graciela García?"

"Lovely. We have two classes together. Next vacation we want to go to Ecuador, where Graci has cousins. Gosh – I want to see some llamas."

"Go to Peru, then," Chilton said. "Go to both countries. I'm all for it. Her parents approve?"

"Yes – they're awfully nice. Sort of like you."

"I'm sure señora García would be flattered. As I remember – and I had dinner

31

with them last week – the señora had not developed gray hair and a gray mustache."

Jimmie laughed. "Silly boy. You know both the señora and Graci look like that marvelous Peruvian singer Yma Sumac. But Uncle John, to go back to my living here – if Vicky could beat off an intruder with a skillet, what couldn't I do with a derringer?"

"You have a derringer, you terrible child? How did you come by it?"

"From a boy in Texas, when I was living there with my aunt. He showed me how to use it – said I ought to have it when I came down here."

"No permit, I suppose?"

"No," Jimmie said. "But how would anybody find it? I keep it hidden in – well, in a package of tampons."

Victoria, at the doorway to the terrace, bringing two liqueur glasses of cognac, halted, startled at the burst of Chilton's laughter. The glance she directed toward Jimmie held gratitude. For making her uncle laugh, Jimmie wondered.

"Bring something for yourself, Vicky," Chilton said. "You don't like cognac – how about a crême de cassis?"

"Thank you, señor. That I would like."

She came back, having undraped the cat,

and sat demurely on a third chair at the table.

We're off the subject, Jimmie thought, but her uncle revived it.

"Vicky, this girl wants to live here. I told her it would add too much to your work."

"Mr. Chilton!"

The address in English, Vicky's first language, sounded harsher than the *señor* which she generally used.

"Mr. Chilton, I had hoped –"

"Aha, another conspiracy," Chilton said. "You know I am trying to arrange for you to have less work so you won't be here alone at night."

"But if Miss Jimmie lived here – I wouldn't be alone. Señor, I would rather have Miss Jimmie than the kitten!"

"You'll have to settle for the kitten," Chilton said, looking at his watch. "And the señorita is going back to the Canal Zone as soon as she finishes her cognac. I'm expecting a visitor. Father Luis."

"I know," Vicky said. "It was on your calendar. I will be here. The poor padre always looks hungry. My nephew will come for me later."

"I wish I could meet Father Luis," Jimmie said.

"You shall some day," her uncle

promised. Tonight – home you go. And not alone. I will drive along behind you until you reach the Canal Zone."

"No!" Jimmie protested. "Nothing's going to happen to me."

"Nothing is," her uncle said. "Ready?"

"Yes, you ogre."

At the outside doorway Vicky held out Jimmie's books, notebooks, handbag, and green scarf. Jimmie hugged her, and went down the stairs ahead of Chilton. From the street, looking up at the white wall of the apartment building, she said, "You'd never guess what's behind these walls – the narrow windows. That's one reason why I like Spanish houses. Secretive."

A half-block down the hill to the right, the Moorish *Presidencia* glowed with its lights. This block was always guarded. A member of the *Guardia Nacional,* leaning against the sea wall outside the yellow house, acknowledged Chilton's greeting.

"Do you hear music?"

"One usually does. From somewhere. Jimmie."

"Yes?"

"That yellow house – the people who live in it – I wouldn't dwell on them if I were you."

Jimmie laughed.

34

"Dwell? What does that mean?"

"I mean don't romanticize the inmates just because they live in an old picturesque Spanish house. They have nothing to offer you."

Jimmie was silent as they passed the house and turned left into the small plaza at whose edge their cars were parked. Colonial white buildings and a church surrounded the plaza on three sides. On the fourth, street lights showed the cream-ocher wall and flower-filled balconies of an apartment house. Music which sounded Arabic came from an open window. This, Jimmie thought, is where I want to live.

She was aware of her uncle's car following; at Fourth of July Avenue, where she would cross into the Canal Zone, she stopped and waited until his car drew beside hers, and waved good-night.

She drove through the serene palm-lined streets of Ancon to Isabel's house on a hillside overlooking dark jungle in the foreground, and farther off, the lighted buildings of an airfield. The house, which had replaced an old building left from the days when the French had worked on a canal, was a modern structure of stucco and glass. It had a patio underneath, edged with croton and bamboo orchids and shaded by

35

a superb royal palm, but Isabel and her family rarely used the patio. Jimmie found them with a guest in the air-conditioned living room, whose sterile chill always shocked her. Isabel, in pale blue linen the color of the rug, sat diagonally across the wide seat of a blue and yellow upholstered chair; Tom, her stepson, was hunched on a hassock; Glenn, her large, genial husband, sat on the sofa beside a guest, Clay Austin; typewritten sheets lay on the coffee table among glasses.

"You disappointed us, dear – we thought you would come earlier," Isabel said.

Clay Austin, gathering up the typewritten sheets, handed them to Glenn and said, "I'll expect you all to come to dinner with me soon. You too, Jimmie, for sure. And think about trying out for that theater guild play."

"I'm too busy at the University," Jimmie said.

"You and the other communists," Tom said.

Clay laughed. "How is your uncle?" he asked Jimmie as he moved toward the hall. "Still deep in Panamanian politics?"

"He's well," Jimmie said.

When Clay had gone, Isabel said, "Jimmie, sit down and let Glenn make you a drink. You look tired. Such long days."

"No drink, thank you."

She sat on an arm of Isabel's chair, ready to leave this room which seemed closed against more than crickets' chirping and the stir of the jungle on the hillside. How different it was from her uncle's living room, open to the bay and the night and permeated with an openness to all the outside world: the books and newspapers, the echoes of study and thought and talk. Isabel's living room might have been transplanted from any house in the States: expensive decorating was evident, avoidance of anything suggesting mental ferment. Or development? Unfair, she thought; Glenn was a substantial conscientious aide to the Governor; Isabel supported her side of the menage by elaborate entertaining. The man who had just left, although occupying a minor administrative position, extended himself through his activities in the community. It's not their fault, she thought, if they never talk about anything that interests me. Even the occasional inevitable discussions of communism had an air-conditioned quality: the term *communist* was still used here as a blanket condemnation.

"Don't you think so, Jimmie?" Isabel said.

37

Glenn, who had been reading from the sheets that Clay had left on the coffee table, spoke before Jimmie had to admit she had not been listening.

"Very sound. Good addition – those statistics about all the benefits Panama has derived. Water supply, highways, health services."

"How is the material to be used?" Jimmie asked.

"But I told you – for the script the tourist guides use when they show visitors the Canal. There's a lot here. The rent we pay – how Panama becomes a – well maybe fifteenth-rate country instead of a thirteenth – because of payments."

"It doesn't sound like good public relations," Jimmie said.

"But it will counteract their propaganda."

"What do you think, Tom?" Jimmie believed the boy had intelligence if not grace or even courtesy.

"To you I guess it sounds putrid," Tom said. "But you've been adopted into their race. Black and communist."

"Tom," his stepmother said. "Unsay that. Jimmie hasn't left our race."

"OK, maybe not. But Jimmie, how many white Panamanians do you know?"

"Plenty," Jimmie said.

Glenn looked at his son.

"Tom, that sort of talk isn't good. You have a right to your opinions. But you mustn't give the idea that you're reflecting me – I wouldn't want you to seem to be quoting me – about racial matters."

"Nuts," Tom said. "I don't have to quote anybody." He stood up and kicked the hassock toward the wall. "I'm going to bed."

"Well," Isabel said, when he had gone, "he doesn't have to be so pugnacious, does he? About everything?"

"It's a phase," Glenn said. "After all, he has to compensate for living out of his own country. Has to feel this *is* part of his country."

"Is it?" Jimmie asked.

"We consider the Zone part of our country," he said. "With all due –"

Isabel giggled. "Glenn, darling, don't make a speech." She got up and drew her fingers over his left cheek. "I've got to go to bed – I'm having people here for lunch tomorrow. Jimmie, why don't you come too?"

"I have to work in the library," Jimmie said. The library – outside, the Cervantes statue – the far blue reach of the hills – but

39

her sister had never cared to see the Universidad Nacional.

In her room she sat on the ledge of a window open to the sound of crickets and the night scents of the jungle.

She thought about the yellow house, and was not at all sure that she had not fallen in love.

4
FATHER LUIS

"So," Chilton thought, on his way home after leaving Jimmie, "I may be being followed. For what it's worth to the follower." He had noticed the small dark car, like any one of several common imports from Europe, shortly before reaching Fourth of July Avenue where he had left Jimmie. Now he saw it again behind him on *Avenida Central* but he did not see it when he reached his apartment building.

Soon afterward his visitor came, Father Luis from the village of Natá in the interior. Four centuries ago the Spaniards had founded a town there; the present village was thought to be the oldest surviving Spanish settlement on the Pacific slope of the Americas. But despite its lineage and the considerable charm of its ancient silver-gray church, Natá was a place of exile for Father Luis, who, for political reasons, had been demoted years ago from his charge in Panama City. On one of his rare trips to the capital he and Chilton had met in a bookstore and had been friends during the eight years since that meeting.

"*Padre,* do you know that seven months have passed since I saw you?"

"Only seven? To me it has seemed much longer."

"Let me take your bag. Books, yes?"

"Some of them, I fear, are on the Index. And a retarded copy of *The New York Times.* But I was fortunate to have time to buy them. The conference to which I was called lasted a long time."

"Have you had dinner?" Chilton asked.

"No, señor, but do not trouble yourself or Victoria."

"For you, *padre,* no trouble would be trouble," Victoria said. While she was slicing cold roast beef, Chilton was searching for strawberries in the refrigerator.

"Why is it so damned hard to find anything in a woman-run refrigerator?"

Amusement brightened Victoria's sternly

41

handsome face, and Father Luis, at the table, laughed. "I do not have that problem. My refrigerator holds very little – ice is scarce – and the boy who does my marketing – he also serves as acolyte – knows nothing about storing food. A neighboring woman sometimes cooks for me. A kind soul and a good cook, but I cannot depend upon her services, for she has seven children."

"Horrors," Chilton said.

"I agree, but do not quote me."

"How do they live? What does the father do?"

"The father," the priest said, "works in a sugar mill. But he makes hardly enough to buy food for his family."

"And you, I suppose," Chilton said, "help them. How?"

"I have a small subsidy for living expenses. We share. And there is always plenty of fruit. Also chickens and eggs."

Chilton found the strawberries, and placed the bowl beside the rolls and butter that Victoria had set out. He added a bottle of sherry.

"A feast," the padre said. "I thank you both. I only wish my poor Negrito – señor, you remember my thin black cat? – could be joining me. The boy who works for me may not remember to feed Negrito. It

42

will be late tonight before he is fed."

Victoria brought a bag containing cans of sardines.

"For Negrito," she said.

"Then you are driving back tonight? I'd like to have you stay here," Chilton said. "Is your car dependable?"

"Very old, but reasonably dependable, unless my superiors have tampered with it."

He spoke jokingly but with an overtone that was not humorous. Chilton stored up the memory of that shade of seriousness.

"I hope your work goes well," the priest said.

"The book – very slowly. And I'm slowing it even more by stopping to write articles for a newspaper chain in the States. In giving my views about the desirability of ratifying the Canal treaties. I have also made a commitment to give one or two talks in the States. I leave next Monday. By the way, did you ever get a telephone?"

"Yes."

"I'd like to let my niece know how to reach you. She is attending the university here. Can't imagine that anything would come up – but she could call my lawyer – and you, if she needed to, while I am away."

"But of course." Father Luis wrote his

43

telephone number in Chilton's address book.

"Incidentally, *padre* – I'm not expecting anything to happen to me, though my work isn't going to win me popularity awards. As you know, I have no ties with any faith. But I have a desire – call it a whim – to have you officiate in the –" he used an English term – "windup. Just a prayer, probably. No fuss. Think you could manage it? Even if I'm not a member of your Church or your parish?"

"I think so. But señor, I find this subject exceedingly distressing."

"We won't pursue it. Tell me about your conferences today."

Father Luis smiled without amusement.

"Conferences, yes, that was what my superiors said when they called me. And when I came, there was much – to use an English word – palaver. Pointless. With a curious undercurrent as though they were trying to tell me something without defining it. Father Sebastian was the principal speaker. A small group, which dwindled until only Father Sebastian and I remained. He, as you know, caused me to be sent to Natá because I could not in conscience join the forces that at that time were working for the return to the presidency of the man who had twice been expelled. You remember."

44

"I remember," Chilton said.

"Señor, would you now think that all the elements in our society would be supporting the Canal Treaties now being considered in the States?"

"No."

"I had supposed so, but I am distant from political involvements. And when I can come to Panama City, I fear I am more interested in going to bookstores than in attending meetings. I speak to you very frankly."

"So what did Father Sebastian propose?"

The doorbell sounded. "Now who –" Chilton frowned. "Who could be coming at ten-thirty?"

He opened the door on its chain, withdrew the chain when he saw a man, a boy, actually, armed with an innocent folded student's theme, bearing on the upper part of the fold a long carefully written comment.

"Mr. Chilton," the boy said in English, "I am Roberto Villalba."

"Come in, Roberto."

"I hesitated to bother you this late – but I saw your lights – and I wanted to return your niece's theme. My brother forgot to return it to her this afternoon."

Another time my prejudices have been too operative, Chilton thought. This boy is in no way like his brother Eduardo except in a

45

certain dark-handsomeness, a tall boy, wearing black-rimmed glasses behind which the eyes showed an intensity and recent immersion in study. Rapt? Go slow, Chilton thought; the boy is a Villalba, with the vivid Villalba beauty.

He introduced Roberto to Father Luis, took the theme, and waved toward a chair.

"Please let me give you a glass of wine to thank you for bringing my niece's paper."

"I thought she should have it because it is an excellent piece of writing," Roberto said. Directness? Half-shyness? Not at all like his brother, Chilton thought.

"No wine, thank you, señor," Roberto said in Spanish. "I have more studying to do."

Chilton, seeing him glance through the room, said, "My niece doesn't live here. She is staying with her sister in the Zone." He thought Roberto looked disappointed.

"Then I should not have troubled you with her theme."

"No trouble. I'll see her in a few days."

"An agreeable boy," the priest said after Roberto had gone.

"You were telling me about your conversation with Father Sebastian."

"There was nothing direct, nothing substantive, in what he said. He masters indirection. But I had the impression that he
46

was suggesting that my return to my charge here might be arranged."

"On certain terms?" Chilton asked.

"Yes. And vaguely he seemed to imply a connection with my attitude toward the Treaties. I may have imagined this; but was there a hint that he wanted me to use whatever influence I have in opposing them? It was puzzling. When I made it clear that I thoroughly supported the Treaties, the talk dried up, and soon he dismissed me, urbanely but definitely."

"Have you heard of a man, or a group called the Condor?"

"But naturally. Mothers frighten unruly children by threatening them with the Condor. A myth. I believed it was."

"Behind the myth," Chilton said, "there is something nasty. Something with tentacles. I have some clues about it and am trying to find out who the faceless man or men are. And what the tentacles have caught."

"Are they connected with our government?"

"Not directly. Not with the leader of the government or with elected officials."

"With any part of the *Guardia Nacional?*"

Chilton hesitated before answering.

47

"I cannot tell. Not yet. And for now – I am sorry you will not be returning to Panama City."

The priest gestured as if dismissing an unimportant idea and rose.

"I am not unhappy at Natá."

"I have some newspapers for you. From Mexico and from England."

"They will be enjoyed."

"And," Chilton added at the door, "I would appreciate your telling me about any more vague offers you receive."

5
CONDOR MEETING

In their bleak, rather damp meeting place, two men sat at a table bare except for three lighted candles. The third man, who should have met with them, lay dying in a hospital in Panama City.

"So," the younger of the two said, "the older man will not be around to see the development of our plans. I must say I am not grieved. He is – was – an old bastard."

The other laughed. "Unquestionably. I am reminded of what the North American

48

President Roosevelt said about President Vargas of Brazil: 'Yes, he is a bastard, but he is *our* bastard.' Before your time. And speaking of age, we have to replace the old man with something much younger."

"Something." The younger man laughed. "As if he was a tool? I have been thinking about the man you have in mind."

"He has been helpful. From the reports that our agents make, he would be sympathetic with our plans. If not entirely by conviction, certainly by rewards. He is intelligent."

"Oh, he's shrewd. I even wonder sometimes whether he knows who we are. For that matter, does Torrijos know?"

"If the Chief of government knows or guesses, he is in no position to say so. Our work has been thorough."

"I know, for I have done most of it."

"That is perhaps disputable – though you have worked admirably. And in a vital area. To be fair, the old bastard gave us a remarkably rich collection of dossiers which have made it possible for us to choose our agents and underlings, none of whom, I am sure, know who we are, although they may make their guesses. This young man –" even in their secret meeting places, the two men habitually did not use names – "by his work

49

for us is so committed to our plans that he could never betray us. Not if he wanted to prosper or live."

The younger man nodded. "True. What about his family though? Is he tight-lipped?"

"As much as anybody else we could find. And there are plenty of ways to control possible indiscretions. Our professional class is poor. You know that. Poor and weak and venal. Also, we need somebody more enterprising, more prominent, more capable of growth than anybody we own in the legislature. And this man, remember, has influence over students. Of all the things we don't want, are student riots that we ourselves do not control."

"We don't want that snooping old North American journalist sniffing into our affairs."

"Let him snoop and sniff," the older man said. "We will deal with him. Have you any suggestions better than mine for our third associate?"

"I know of a man with the qualifications that we need. I am not often wrong in making judgments like this. He is a ruthless man who could be bought away from his present connections."

"What are his present connections?"

"You would probably consider them an insuperable deterrent. Remember, though, that I am judging the man as a working tool. He now works in the Administration of the Canal Zone."

"A North American?" The older man spoke scornfully. "Impossible. We are Panamanians working for Panama."

"And ourselves," the younger man muttered.

"Understood. Since I absolutely veto your ridiculous suggestion, have you anyone else to nominate?"

"No."

"Then we decide? Or do you want to go to the hospital and extract a vote from the old man – if he is still alive?"

"Probably he's too far gone. No, I will not object any further. Let's get out of this place. I don't like it."

"Too much like the Catacombs?"

The younger man shrugged. "Too much like the dungeons of Fuerte San Lorenzo."

6
THE SILVER COIN

Chilton returned from the United States to Panama some weeks later. After appearing before a Senate committee, being interviewed by reporters for three newspapers, giving talks at University forums, and having the satisfaction of seeing the first of the two treaties approved by the Senate, he had barely time to visit the president of the company that had contracted to publish his new book. The manuscript was far behind schedule, and even now he could not promise its delivery by a certain date because he had gaps to fill and substantiations to make of the material in several chapters.

"With all the tonnage of documents you must already have," the publisher had said, "I'd think you could complete a half dozen exposés off the bat."

"There are always new developments. And the book is not an exposé. I would call it an analysis. It cuts in several directions. For and against policies and attitudes in this country and in Latin America, with focus on Panama.

Not only concerning the Canal issue."

"You're the man to do it. I don't know of anybody else who could. Get the manuscript to us as soon as you can – even in installments."

"I'll do my best," Chilton had promised.

"You are tired," Victoria said now on his return.

"Yes, rather. Not much time for food and nothing as good as your cooking." He settled himself in his favorite leather chair, waiting for the Scotch and soda that Victoria would bring him. An ivory-colored kitten sprang into his lap.

"That," Victoria said, placing his glass on a table beside him, "is Frangi. After you said we could have a kitten, I got him from a neighbor. I hope he won't be a trouble."

"Not at all. He looks like a good type. Hey – you been feeding him Scotch? He wants my drink. Is he an alcoholic?"

"No. He just wants to help welcome you home."

"Have you heard from Jimmie?"

"She came in last Thursday and asked me to remind you of the cocktail party at her sister's on April 16. A week from tomorrow. She is busy having tests."

"Damn, I'd forgotten," Chilton said. "Well, what's new here?"

53

Victoria brought his mail.

"Father Luis telephoned last week. He thought you would be back and wanted to hear about your trip. I asked whether he got home all right that night after he was here. But he didn't. A truck came around a curve very fast. He had to drive off the road, and his car broke down."

"How far from Natá?"

"About three miles."

Chilton frowned. "Did he have to walk those three miles?"

"Yes. He said he didn't mind, but he hasn't been able to get his car repaired."

"I should have tried harder to have him stay overnight here. He needs a car. Probably doesn't have money to pay for repairs. I must do something about that. Trouble is – he's so independent. Gentle man but determined. Well, I'll think of something."

"You will think of something," Victoria said confidently. To divert him from worry about his friend, she chattered about what Chilton thought of as the maids' underground.

"My young friend Laura works in the Zone. Maybe you'll see her – she's going to help Mrs. Furniss's maid at the party. Her boss never talks to her the way you talk to me. She thinks he isn't used to maids, or

54

maybe doesn't like Negroes. He dyes his hair gray. Why would a man do that?"

"To look older, more dignified. Who's her boss?"

"Somebody working for Mr. Furniss and the Governor of the Zone. She says his natural hair color is red. He had to answer the phone one day when he had taken out the old dye and was going to use the new gray. And it was red. And Paula, the maid next door at the Villalbas, finally got paid. They hadn't paid her for over two months. She says she wouldn't have stayed, but for Mr. Roberto. She likes him and says the other two are always making him do things for them. Now they pay her – and give her something extra. She says they've paid all their bills. She can't understand how; even if they got paid for their coffee, it wouldn't be that much. They had a lot owing. She says Mr. Eduardo must have robbed a bank."

In his investigation, Chilton did not usually probe for information from servants, both because he disapproved of the method and because answers from direct questioning were likely to be pointed toward what the questioner wanted to hear or protective of an employer. When information was volunteered, however, he received it and often found it crucially helpful. He remembered a chance talk, in a cantina in the Chorillo district, with the gardener on the estate of a former president. The gardener had, on his own initiative, provided names of supporters of the former discredited president, who was seeking reelection, and dates of meetings. Which reminds me, Chilton thought, that the shipment of roller skates I ordered for children in the club Father Luis had once run in the Chorillo district had not arrived. One of Father Luis's chief regrets in his banishment had been the halting of his work in what was perhaps the poorest part of the city.

Now, considering Victoria's relayed information about Eduardo Villalba, Chilton reviewed what he had learned about Eduardo's father from Tomás, a junior member of the lawyer García's firm, who sometimes did research for him with the lawyer's approval. It was widely known that the present Villalbas attributed their penury to their father and brother's excessive honesty in refusing to take advantage of secret information about a government road-building project. But the fact was that the senior Villalba had not refused; he had been outwitted by another land-buyer. The low state of the family's finances was due to outpouring of money by Eduardo's father on the maintenance of mistresses and other non-inheritable luxuries.

In looking through his mail, Chilton found a note from Victoria, whose written productions did not match the correctness of her speech:

Mr. Chilton somebody named Clif phones he wanted to see you but cant go back to the cantina because theyre after him. He will phone or come here.

Who, Chilton pondered, was "after" Cliff, the homesick young soldier he had met in the Chorilla district? M.P.s, probably: Chorilla was off-limits to personnel at the United States bases in the Canal Zone. He had argued the boy not to desert. Their meeting had taken place on one of Chilton's visits to Chorillo to watch for signs that bands of impoverished men were being armed and trained by a political leader planning insurrection. Through Father Luis he had made contact with informants about the temper of the district; he also helped a few destitute families whom the priest had aided in the past.

This coming week, Chilton decided, he would go to Chorillo again. He made a note in his own code of abbreviations (which often

57

he could not read); thought for a moment, then added another note: "Resee C.G. on any sh. mvmnts. to harb. Coc coast." That harbor that he knew of on the coast of Coclé province was secluded enough to shelter ships carrying contraband. Arms? He would talk with a friend in the Coast Guard.

He took the note into the kitchen and asked Vicky, "Did that boy – Cliff – say anything else when he telephoned?"

"No. He sounded mighty unhappy, though."

"He is unhappy," Chilton said. "Young soldier at a base in the Canal Zone. Thinking of deserting. I met him in a cantina in Chorillo." He smiled. "Don't look shocked, Vicky. I often go into Chorillo but not to carouse."

"Not a good place to go. Worst place in this city. Mr. Chilton, I don't think you ought to go down there at night alone."

"I'm not alone – thousands of Panamanians live there. I go down there, Vicky, to keep an eye on what's happening. To see whether any politician is organizing bands of men to start a riot. It's happened before. Plenty of people to be bought up, given a little training, some guns – what *have* you got in that oven? Stupefying good smell."

"Chicken in white wine. A new recipe."

Wearing the apricot-colored blouse Chilton had bought for her at Saks Fifth Avenue during his trip north, Victoria seemed to be watching with unusual interest as he sorted his mail and read selected parts. When he came to the bottom of the pile, he understood why. A slip of paper taped to a small tissue-wrapped disc, bore, in Vicky's writing, the words:

Mr. Chilton, this is for your collection.

V.

He removed the tissue and found a silver coin, a Spanish *real* from the sixteenth century.

"Vicky, you are a jewel! But this must have been very expensive."

"No, Mr. Chilton. I got it in a dirty little old shop near the market."

"It's great! I'll put it into my collection right away." He tried to read the date, which even Victoria's polishing had not made legible. The likeness of Philip II on the obverse, however, was clear and beautiful.

In his study he took from a wall the red and blue *mola*, one of the cotton-cloth appliqué decorations made by San Blas Indians, which covered the door of his small safe. He opened the safe and brought out the cardboard box that held his ancient Spanish

59

coins, most of them silver, with a few gold doubloons. One of the latter he himself had found on the old Gold Trail along which mule trains had carried Peruvian riches from the Pacific to the Spanish treasure fleet in the Caribbean.

He spent a few minutes admiring the beauty of the coins, all but hearing them ring on some enormous carved walnut table or counter, letting himself imagine ways in which they had been spent, and who had lost them, perhaps in an ambush in the crossing of the Isthmus three or four hundred years ago. Indians? Bands of *maroons* – the outlaw Negroes, or inland-turned pirates like Morgan, who had burned and sacked Panama Vieja. Come now, he thought, let's not get carried away. I must get a coin album and organize these. I grow less and less systematic.

As he sometimes did, he left the box on his desk, where he could enjoy them. He closed the safe and rehung the *mola*. At least, he thought, I am fairly systematic about storing materials.

He now limited the contents of his safe to the coin collection, the immediate chapters and notes for a current project, money for emergency use, and copies of his will and the memorandum to his lawyer ordering the immediate destruction in case of his death, of all manuscripts, documents, and notes stored in a bank vault.

With amusement he remembered the monumental masses of material he had kept in the apartment when he had been writing for a newspaper a series of articles on Latin American politics. Even in his one attempt at fiction, a historical novel based on the life of Balboa, he had sorely taxed Victoria by inundating the apartment with books and notes and manuscript. She had been near mutiny on finding Chapter 11 of the book, dismembered, in the linen closet. Odd thing, he thought: that ruddy novel had surprised him and his publisher by selling well.

He wondered whether Jimmie had read it. Not, certainly, at the time of publication eight years ago, for she would have been only ten, eleven years old. A lovely child, he thought, even if preoccupied with boys who gave her derringers and the brilliantly handsome dark descendant of Villalbas, who, he thought, never skipped a generation in a long line of brilliantly handsome scions. How did they do it? A subject for an article? By now would some of the Villalba traits have been filtered clean? He was doubtful, even remembering the impression Roberto

Villalba had made the night he had come to the apartment.

7
LAUGHTER FROM THE JUNGLE

Clay Austin scowled when he found the foyer of his apartment in Ancon lighted Sunday night around nine when he returned from the cocktail party at the Furniss's.

"You'll be late getting home," he said to his maid Laura.

"My husband will meet me. I thought you might like some dinner – coffee anyway?"

"No. You can go. Right away."

"I'll leave the percolator connected – so you can have it later."

I don't care what you do, he thought; just leave me alone.

He heard Laura's low voice telephoning, and presently she came from the darkened kitchen to stand hesitantly in the foyer in the half-light from lamps there and in the living room. Her hair, released from the neat roll in which she had worn it earlier, masked the right side of her forehead and obscurely shadowed the white of her uniform, covering the angles of her shoulders and by its duskiness bringing into pale relief the ivory beige of her skin. But it was the gesture of her right hand toward her throat, the fingers turned outward, apologetic, tentatively asking to be allowed to speak, to justify her presence, that made Clay shiver as if he were seeing a ghost. He was.

The vague soft beauty, the features of the face dimmed by the black torrent of hair, the gentleness, almost supplication of the attitude in the wash of low light, broke through the layers of induced forgetting and stabbed a fresh wound in the old one in his memory.

He turned to switch on a brighter lamp, and when he looked back, he heard the front door close. He was alone. He had been spared whatever Laura had wanted to say. At one level in his mind he knew that she had wanted only to offer some service. At a lower level he hated her for what she had made him remember.

Outside the living room window a jungle creature laughed without mirth.

He poured bourbon, took the glass to his desk, turned on a brighter light.

The jungle voice laughed again.

Something flicked against the wide screened window, almost the width of the wall. He threw the bourbon into the screen. Liquid dripped down on the Chinese rug.

"A bat," he thought. "A damned squeaking bat."

8
LAURA

Laura walked hand in hand with Antonio, her husband, through Santa Ana Plaza in Panama City. The night was gentle, romantic. Antonio, who drove a bus in Panama City, had worked today although it was Sunday. He had reached their apartment in time to shower and dress in clean clothes before Laura telephoned, and then had gone out to meet her at the wire wall which separated part of Ancon, in the Canal Zone, from the city. They had bought *empanadas* and mango ice from a cart and were now on their way to a bench among the palm trees in the plaza.

As usual, they talked to each other in English, Laura's first language. Her great-grandparents had been brought from Jamaica to work on the Canal. Antonio's father had been Panamanian, his mother a

San Blas Indian. He spoke English but wanted to make it more fluent.

"Another ice, *querida?*"

"No, thank you, Antonio. Would you like me to cook *arroz con pollo* tomorrow night? I do not expect to be late."

"Yes, and I will bring you a surprise."

"You are enough surprising," Laura said.

"And so," Antonio said, as if continuing what they often talked of, "some more savings – then we can afford to work fewer hours – and *then* we enter the University. Not much longer. If we take courses at night – but you are not to work too hard by day – then I will study about running a business. A small one. Something to do with food, no? Everybody eats. And you – you can study your languages and become a secretary – or at least a housekeeper at one of the embassies. And you can take the art courses you want."

Both had completed high school with records high enough to ensure admittance to the University. The world of their dreams shone before them. They agreed: no children now, perhaps ever. They felt no incompleteness in their lives.

"Lovely, lovely," Laura said. "High school – that was where we met – the University – we will meet again there."

"No more trouble with that Furniss boy?" Antonio asked as they started back toward their home.

"No, I slapped him hard. Celia, Mrs. Furniss's maid, never has trouble with him."

"Celia isn't you, *chica*. She must be twenty, thirty years older than you. Does Señor Austin bother you?"

"No. I think he doesn't like me – doesn't want a maid. Or maybe he doesn't like Negroes. But he has to have a maid. He is what the North Americans call a big wheel. Sometimes he makes me feel like a zombie – am I a zombie, Antonio?"

"If you are, I love zombies."

At a street corner they were held up by a scurrying group of men, some carrying sticks, others clutching long objects under ragged shirts. The band turned off *Avenida Central* toward *Via Francia,* the wide esplanade overlooking the sea.

"What are they doing?" Laura asked uneasily.

"Training for a riot? Who knows? In Chorillo they are always ready – but who can blame them, Laurita? They are starving."

"So that whoever pays them – but why should there be riots now? The Canal

Treaties? The first one has passed. Why would there be riots?"

"There are people who don't want the Treaties. You have heard of the Condor?"

"That. Is there a Condor?"

Before Antonio could answer, the stars disappeared and one of the sudden torrents of the rainy season exploded. They ran along *Avenida Central,* dodging other running figures, and arrived at their apartment dripping and laughing.

The apartment was very small, but it had a little balcony on which Laura grew flowering plants.

9
VISITORS TO CHILTON

The devil of it is, Chilton thought, I've relied too much on notes and documents, not enough on memory. When something rings a bell out of the damned long corridors of the past, I don't always remember who, what, when, or where. Only have an impression of the kind of circumstance the bell rings about. Far enough back, and the circumstances would be dark, sordid, for early on, I started as a crime reporter. For that matter, a lot of more recent facts elude me, but with them I can remember a category and consult my notes, which Raúl García has catalogued by topics, names, and years.

For almost twenty years Raúl has been his most trusted friend. Chilton was pleased that Jimmie and Graciela García, classmates at the University, seemed devoted to each other. An assistant in Raúl's law firm had done valuable work for him. I will try to have lunch with Raúl tomorrow, he thought. Meanwhile – he frowned. He was proud of being able to pin down to one or sometimes two states any accent of a North American. And he could usually identify the nationality of a Latin American, but the accent and speech habits of a man he had met that afternoon puzzled him. Natural speech overlaid with training of some kind? And those stupid bells that this man had caused to ring – why the hell couldn't they tell why they were ringing?

The party had been better than he had expected. His nieces had looked edible, Isabel in lavender, Jimmie in white; Glenn's white suit must have been London-tailored. The other guests, even knowing Chilton's political views, had been cordial, including the bland Governor and his rather attractive wife. No one except Isabel had reacted visibly to his Ohio comparison, which he would not have repeated if the Governor's wife had not brought up the subject. So he had said again, "If you lived in Ohio, how would you feel if your state were cut in two by a giant ditch controlled by a foreign power?"

"I remember hearing that quoted," she said. "But why Ohio?"

"Because the man I was talking with came from Ohio. It would be true for any other state."

At the door when he was leaving, Jimmie had kissed him.

"Thanks for coming. See you soon? I'm cramming chemistry. Horrible stuff."

"Don't forget English history. And take physics sometime."

"I'll be damned if I do," Jimmie said cheerfully.

Now, in his study, he planned for the coming week. He must call Father Luis – that could not be put off.

Although Victoria's Sundays were supposed to be free, she was indefatigable in coming to the apartment long enough to prepare dinner. Tonight, Chilton found lamb chops and peas and rolls and a pot of coffee staying hot on the electric heating tray. In front of it a note said, "Mr. Chilton, shrimp salad in refrigerator and banana ice cream in freezer. Frangi sends love. V."

He poured Scotch and drank a silent toast to Victoria. Before finishing the drink – he had had only one Scotch at Isabel's party and none of the irrelevant hors d'oevres which he loathed – he answered the doorbell and found Roberto Villalba bearing a bouquet of purple flowers.

"These grow on our terrace," Roberto said. "I thought you might like some."

A move, Chilton wondered, to ingratiate himself with me because of my niece? But as on their first meeting, the simplicity and directness of Roberto's expression, of his whole manner, were disarming.

"I would indeed," Chilton said. "Come in. I'm having a Scotch. Will you have one?"

"I would like to. But I have to finish writing a paper by tomorrow morning."

"Sometime when you aren't busy," Chilton said, "come back and we'll talk about Coclé. I assume you've been doing some excavating. The other day I happened to be driving in the area and saw a new-looking wall around some of the old digs."

"A wall?" Roberto said. "I haven't been out there for ages. I'd be glad to come back here to talk about Coclé or anything else."

I like the boy, Chilton thought, as he put the purple flowers into a jar of water. Never expected to like a Villalba. Maybe by their charm they have always accomplished their purposes. Still, I like Roberto.

He finished his drink and glanced through newspapers that he had not read in the morning. So, he thought, the old wily politician, the twice expelled former President of Panama, had died. And with him whatever he knew of the secrets of the Condor. Some of the leads in Chilton's investigations had pointed to the old man as a likely Condor or member of the Condor fraternity. If he were to be replaced, would the Condor operations undergo a change? I must send somebody to the funeral, he thought, to see if any of my suspects attend; though the old man's celebrity would probably draw too many people to make such observations productive.

He ate the first part of the dinner Victoria had prepared and stopped to make notes on what had penetrated the swarm of ideas through which his mind groped. He was constructing a short context, as he usually did, in order to bury the significance of any one part of a jotting, when the doorbell rang again.

10
THE SNAKESKIN BELT

At first, up there in the apartment, Cliff's mind had emptied, so that he could not think. The way something stops bleeding, that was the way the edges of his thoughts had come together. To get away – from this horror – out of this uniform – out of the city – out of the country. He had been in enough trouble before tonight.

To remove the snakeskin belt that held the dreadful and pitiable figure upright in a chair at the street window nauseated him. The belt had been fastened across the chest of the figure and then to the chairback. Another belt of plain black leather held the shoulders. Even without the snakeskin belt, the figure retained its position. Rigor, Cliff thought. That snakeskin belt – he knew it would not have been John Chilton's, not that slimy slippery thing more animate than the poor body. That belt might identify an owner. The other could have belonged to anybody.

From a box on the desk he took six coins. If ever – but no use not to think of repaying his friend. And he himself had nothing, no money to start his escape from the city, the country. Even through the belt of his trousers he felt the dankness of the snakeskin.

He was not religious, but he knelt for a moment beside the figure in the chair and felt rather than prayed, felt grief and affection. I have never known anybody like you, he thought.

The guard had seen him go in, could not have noticed that Cliff had found the street door of the apartment house unlocked, as he had found the door to Chilton's apartment on the second floor. So it did not matter if he were seen going out.

The guard was sauntering up from the Presidencia. Cliff waited until the man was near the apartment, then waved up toward the window where the figure in the chair was visible in the light from a lamp beyond.

If only, he thought with agony, if only that figure would wave back to him.

The guard glanced up at the window and then returned the salute Cliff gave him.

"Buenas noches, amigo."

"Good night," Cliff answered. He made himself walk slowly toward the square beyond the yellow house, where lights showed on the sea side, on patios that

73

overhung the water. People, he thought: lucky people. At home. He sat on a bench, holding his head in his hands. Why, he wondered, had he enlisted, why had he asked for training at the jungle survival school so far from South Dakota? Adventure in a foreign country? It had been hell. Early April now – at home his father would be getting ready to plant wheat. In another month or two violets would bloom. His mother would be planning her vegetable garden. His favorite sister, married to the operator of a filling station, would be having her baby. And Cloudy, the white shepherd dog, would be pursuing his feud with the postman.

His pass had expired at midnight. The time was now a little after one. The MPs would be looking for him. He took off his uniform jacket and cap and pushed them down into a trash can. His fingerprints were in the living room and the study of the apartment; he would be hunted now for more than desertion. How could he get out of this country? On foot, through the jungle toward Costa Rica? The way to the Colombian border would be worse; and Colombia is the wrong direction from home.

From where he sat he could look down at the sea beyond the marina. A fishing boat would be more likely to pass along the shore here; the marina was crowded with yachts. Daylight wouldn't come until about six. Back on his left he could still see the lights in the yellow house, those enviable lights in the big house where rich people lived.

The rain, which had been falling heavily when he went to the apartment, was only a sprinkle now. His undershirt was soaked more from sweat than from rain. If only, he thought, he had gone to the apartment earlier. But he had been at a cantina, trying to decide what to do. And he had thought, later, that Chilton would not be asleep, or if awakened, would not refuse to see him. All he could do now, he thought, was to stay here until nearer dawn, when he would go down to the embankment and watch for a fishing boat which he would hail, hoping that the fishermen would take him somewhere out of the city, perhaps north toward Costa Rica.

After the rain stopped, a chill dampness pressed through him. Someone had left a newspaper on the bench; he unfolded it, wrapped it over his chest and shoulders, and huddled against the back of the bench. Unexpectedly he slept. When he woke, the night was still dark; but he saw the lights of a boat heading toward the sea. He climbed

down the embankment, jumped into the
water, and swam toward the boat, shouting,
"Help! Help!" What was the Spanish word?
He remembered. *"Socorro! Socorro!"*

11
OVAL OF WHITENESS

Roberto was trying to keep his mind on
Cervantes. Through the open casement
windows he saw the lights of the boats
moored in the marina, and beyond, the
spangling along the opposite curve of the
city. Ilangilang flowers on the trees outside
the lower patio smelled like the perfume a
beautiful woman would wear: someone with
gold-chestnut hair and blue-violet eyes.
Gosh, he thought, in American; and peeled
a banana.

"Roberto," Teresa, swathed in a black
dressing gown, stood at the patio door.
"Chico," she mourned, "please find me
some cognac. I have the most dire headache.
I have rung – but God knows where the
servants are."

Obediently, Roberto went downstairs and
searched the liquor cabinet.

76

"No cognac," he said to Teresa, who had followed him. "It's too late to buy any."

"Well – there is a light in the apartment of señor Chilton. You could borrow some from him, no?"

"But it's almost two o'clock."

"So I suffer the rest of the night. Oh yes, I have tried aspirin. For these headaches nothing helps but cognac."

"But I have already interrupted señor Chilton once tonight."

"So interrupt the old one again. Probably he doesn't need much sleep. I do."

"All right," Roberto agreed reluctantly. He went up to his room, put on his gray bathrobe over his pajamas, huaraches on his feet, and went downstairs and out into the area between the yellow house and the apartments. The police guard, halfway down the street toward the Presidencia, turned and waved. Roberto rang the bell at the street entrance to the apartment building. There was no answer to the signal it would have made in Chilton's apartment. He tried the door, which was unlocked, and went upstairs. Again, there was no answer to his ring.

"Señor Chilton," he called. "Are you there?"

No response. Roberto went down again

to the street. The guard was not in sight; probably, Roberto thought, receiving nourishment in the kitchen of the Presidencia.

"I am sorry, *tia*," he said on his return. "Señor Chilton did not answer the bell."

"Well, thank you, *chico*," his aunt said. "I hear Eduardo arriving – perhaps he will think of something."

Eduardo swept into the hallway, quickly kissed his aunt, and patted Roberto's shoulder.

"Out on the patio," he said. "We will have a nightcap together. The rain has stopped."

"Yes – maybe a Scotch and soda –" Teresa said.

"You, my grubby little one," Eduardo said to his brother. "I suppose you have been studying all this time? Come along and help me make the drinks."

In the kitchen he set out the glasses, then, thinking of something he wanted to tell Teresa, left Roberto to finish making the drinks. Roberto grumbled soundlessly. Still, he thought, it is worth something to have them in good humor.

"Cool, cool, out here," Teresa said. "Eduardo, see how graceful the *Isla* looks. Let's board her and take a cruise."

"She is under charter," Eduardo said. He sat on the rail, holding his glass toward the light from an iron lantern, slowly swirling the ice cubes. "Sometime when she is free we will sail away – perhaps to Tahiti. Would you like that, *hermanito?*"

"Yes, if the *Isla* doesn't smell of fish."

"The trade winds will cleanse her," Eduardo said. "And what a mind you have – no poetry."

"Don't be too sure," Teresa said, unexpectedly defending Roberto, who wondered if she were well. But in a moment he was reassured, for in her usual querulous manner, she ordered him to bring her a wrap. In her room, stormily disordered and scented from her perfumes, he brought out a white lace and wool shawl and placed it around her shoulders. She caught his hand, pressed it, and said, "Thank you, Roberto."

It's the millennium, he thought, and felt sorry for her. So long without the husband, whom from what he had heard she had intensely loved – who had died in an automobile accident fifteen years ago. Roberto could not remember him but had heard that he had been irresistibly handsome, a gambler, perhaps ne'er-do-well. Fifteen years – what a time. And she must have had many suitors during those years.

He went back to his chair, wishing that Jimmie could know his aunt and Eduardo in one of their untheatrical interludes. And then – my god, how am I going to have enough money – enough to marry Jimmie? I am twenty-one – with nothing except half-ownership in some land, in a few crops – the coffee, the pineapples – their sale doesn't amount to much. He worried at a lock of hair on his forehead. I can get a teaching job at the University when I graduate this summer. Will it be enough for two people to live on? No. Damn and blast. Get a grip on yourself, he thought. I'll take a job street-cleaning. And how would Jimmie like that? Not at all. My ancestors owned a fifth of Peru in the sixteenth century. Wrong? But there it was. Another ancestor was an advisor to Charles V – a member of the Order of the Golden Fleece. None of that helps now. And probably shouldn't. Why do I feel an unreasonable affection for that Emperor and for his son, Philip II? What a snarl of contradictions: I write for a leftist independent newspaper, but I feel loyalty to the Hapsburgs. Much closer to them than to any ancestors on my mother's side.

Eduardo, still sitting on the rail, hoped the others had not heard him gasp. His hands gripped the rail, his glass gritted on the iron. A ghost? What was that oval of whiteness that showed intermittently in the water below him, near the *Isla*'s mooring? He tried to identify it as a patch of light from the searchlight the *Guardia* kept on the roof of a building halfway down the hill toward the Presidencia. It was not being rotated. A steady stream of light pointed into the marina, far to the left of the *Isla*. He closed his eyes, opened them again. The whiteness was still bobbing up and down in a horrible travesty of carefree movement. A human face?

The tide, gentled in the sheltering marina, came in strongly enough to sway the craft on their lines. Eduardo saw a dark object below the white oval: both the darkness and the whiteness shifted position with the motion of the *Isla.*

He must go down into the water, must dislodge whatever was caught in the mooring. The *Isla* must not be involved in anything leading to investigation of any kind.

If only Teresa and Roberto would finish their drinks and go to bed. They seemed to be tasting, sipping, slowly. Teresa was relaxed in her chair, Roberto leaned forward resting an elbow on his knee and looking up thoughtfully at the stars. From where they sat they would not see the *Isla.*

Eduardo drained his glass. "It seems chilly out here."

"No, it is pleasant," Teresa said. "I am considering another drink. A small one."

"Please, no," Eduardo said. "I am afraid your headache might come back. Couldn't you sleep now?"

"Before long. Roberto is not sleepy; he is counting the stars."

He can't go on much longer, Eduardo thought; by now he must have had time to count hundreds, thousands.

When Teresa and Roberto finally left the patio, Eduardo forced himself to wait a few more minutes before he hurried to his room, stripped, put on swimming trunks, and went down to the basement door, which opened on steps leading into the water. If the guard on the roof to the left, beyond the apartment house, did not choose in the next few minutes to send his flash beam in this direction – *Maria santissima*, restrain the guard, he thought, as he stepped into the water. What am I doing here – but I know too well what I am doing. The water closed over his body; he struck out toward the mooring line, toward the horrible bobbing white face.

His legs struck the body that belonged to the face; even if the guard had turned the flashlight to the right, the sheer of the *Isla* would have thrown a protecting screen. Eduardo groped at the figure; the line ran under its arms, securely fastening it upright. He released the bind of the rope, caught the slack weight by the shoulders; a heavy man, the *Isla*'s riding light showed gray hair. Holding the mooring line with one hand and pushing the dragging weight of the drowned man below water, he hailed the ship.

"Rita!" he called softly, then more loudly, "Miguel!"

No one answered. *Pendejo,* he swore silently. Then Miguel answered, *"Qué pasa?"*

"Where is Rita?"

"Asleep."

"I want you to take the *Isla* away from here. This moment. Up the coast. To the usual harbor."

"But the repairs –"

"We can't wait for repairs. Take her out immediately."

"Not reasonable," Miguel said sullenly.

"But necessary."

"What are you doing, there in the water?"

"How else do I communicate with you, *estúpido?*"

"But I have worked all day, doing what

I could on the repairs – do I work all night, too?"

"Yes, if I order you to," Eduardo said. "Call Rita."

"That I will not do. She would be angry as a mad boar. But I will take out the *Isla*."

Treading water, holding down the drowned man, Eduardo waited until he heard the *Isla*'s engine start, and then began to swim, towing the lifeless weight away from the yellow house, toward the approach to the apartment building, which had water steps leading to a basement door. He could let go, let the corpse float free – but if he were seen, it would be worse than if he tried to bring it somewhere ashore.

A ray of light grazed the water and moved outward, near the shore. The guard. Eduardo pushed the white revealing face of the body under the water, submerged his own face, rode shoreward on the drive of his last stroke, drifted, then reached the steps at the apartment house.

The tide swung the body away. The flashlight was moving, picking out the slanting masts of a boat, then tracing a line inward, fell on him.

He raised an arm, shouting to the guard.

"Help! Help! A man has drowned!"

12
SCENT OF THE LAST CIGAR

Around four on the following morning when the telephone rang, Jimmie, a light sleeper, answered the extension near her room. Less than a minute later Isabel came from her room to find the receiver dropped from the stand, the connection open. She spoke then listened.

Her screams were still sounding when Jimmie, pulling a sweater over slacks, ran past her to the stairway, down to the ground floor, out to her car.

From the empty dark streets of Ancon she drove at unmeasured speed across the boundary into *Avenida Central,* unaware of lights, of occasional cars, along a short cross street into *Avenida Norte,* past the brilliantly lit *Presidencia* toward the apartment, impelled by a frantic urgency, only half believing what Roberto's voice on the telephone had told her, half accepting what he had said – and that half in an engulfment of horror and grief.

Cars of the *Guardia* crowded the street in
85

front of the apartment building. The men let her go through and up to the apartment, where a guard at the door took her hand and led her into the living room.

"Where – *where* is he?"

Roberto, skin-drenched in white slacks and shirt – she saw him first as he came to meet her, with Eduardo, in bathing trunks, dripping, dark wet hair capped over his head and forehead, and behind both of them a woman whose black hair fell over the shoulders of a blue dressing gown. Three members of the *Guardia* stood inside the front door and the door to the terrace.

"He isn't here?"

Roberto put his arm across her shoulders.

"Not here. He has been taken away."

"It isn't true! It can't –"

The woman in blue put her arm around Jimmie.

"It is true," she said.

"Then tell me," Jimmie appealed to Roberto. "How could it – what happened –"

"Jimmie. What happened – we don't know. Only that around three Eduardo saw – a whiteness, a face – in the water of the marina between this building and our house. Something that should not have been there among the boats moored or at anchor."

"My nephew dived into the water." The aunt was speaking. "We heard his calls for help – Roberto dove in too."

"Jimmie," Eduardo said, "we brought him out. Your uncle. It was too late. He had been caught in the mooring line of a boat."

Jimmie sank into a chair near the terrace door and closed her eyes. When she opened them, Roberto was holding a glass of brandy. "Please take this."

She felt cold as if she herself had come drenched from the water of the marina, too cold to be more than superficially warmed by the brandy.

"I must call Victoria."

"I will call her," Roberto said. "You know the number?"

She gave him the number, heard him telephoning, and listening to the dreadful finality of what he had to tell Victoria, shuddered. Drops of brandy spilled from her glass.

"Victoria will be here within a half-hour," Roberto said. "Your sister will come?"

"Yes."

One of the Guardia came to her.

"Señorita, I am Captain Reyes. I suffer for you. But I must talk with you."

"Wait at least until the sister comes,"

Teresa Villalba said imperiously. "The child is not going away."

No, Jimmie thought, I am not going away. She was aware of the faint odor of the last cigar that her uncle had smoked. For a moment the familiarity of the scent made her feel close to her uncle but was too deeply a part of her grief to bring comfort.

She left the chair and walked slowly into her uncle's study. The captain started to follow her, but Eduardo curtly ordered him to leave her alone. On her uncle's desk lay a sheet of paper from a small pad bearing a few lines in her uncle's writing, an unfinished paragraph, the last words he had written. Her eyes did not focus well, she would read the lines later. She put the pad into the pocket of her sweater.

13
DEPARTURE OF THE ISLA

Roberto could not remember when he and the other two members of his family had lunched together as they were doing this Monday, early because they had had no breakfast and almost no sleep during Sunday night. This departure from custom was further marked by a suspension of the alliance between his aunt and Eduardo: there was no bantering at Roberto's expense.

At another time, Roberto would have found pleasure in the companionship but today he was still suffering from the shock of Chilton's death, grieving for Jimmie, and uneasy because of an interrogation from Captain Reyes, who had been quick to trace the purple flowers to their origin, had concluded from their freshness that they had probably been delivered the evening before, and had found Roberto's fingerprints on the door, which he must have touched on his second visit to the apartment. Roberto worried also about Eduardo. As he remembered, Eduardo had not gone to the terrace after he and Teresa and Roberto had separated for the night; but Eduardo must have seen the figure in the water from the terrace while the three were together. Why, Roberto wondered, had Eduardo not immediately taken action? And why had the *Isla* so suddenly left the harbor before the repairs could have been finished?

He had asked Eduardo about the *Isla*, and Eduardo had said that he supposed the charterers had decided to take her out.

"Before daylight?"

Eduardo shrugged.

"And who are the charterers?"

"Oh, a party of fishermen. Not commercial. By the way, I learned several things from one of the police. Reyes of course believes that you went to the apartment last night."

"But I told him so," Roberto said.

"He thinks it odd that you should have taken a bunch of flowers to Chilton. Why did you?"

"Because I thought he would like them. He *did* seem to like them."

"Well, tone down, *chico*. I'm not suggesting any abnormality. And anyway, there may have been another visitor. Fingerprints at various places. Victoria said that Chilton might have been expecting a visit from a soldier he was trying to help. The prints are being checked through Washington. There was no forced entry; Chilton must have known any – or all – visitors and released the door chain. Victoria found one thing: part but not all of a collection of old and valuable coins that Chilton had left on his desk was missing."

Now, at lunch, the maid Paula brought a plate of *plátano* slices to Roberto.

"I'll have some *plátanos*, Paula," Teresa said.

"I am sorry, señora. There are no more," Paula said, retreating into the kitchen.

"To you, Roberto, the *plátanos* are served! But why?"

"I am sure that Paula has no hidden motives," Eduardo said. "She is a model of rectitude."

"And how do you know that?" his aunt asked.

Roberto gave her the *plátanos*.

"What I haven't told either of you," Teresa said, "is that my headache last evening was probably caused by the unfortunate Chilton himself. He was standing at the wall looking down at the water when I came out. He stopped me to say that the *Isla* looked attractive with its lights, and he asked whether I sometimes made trips on board. I gave an indefinite answer, for what concern could it have been of his? I do not – did not like his observing, his ferreting. No doubt he kept fieldglasses at every window."

"I doubt it," Roberto said. Teresa, ignoring him, continued.

"I wonder what will happen to his papers."

"We will find out," Eduardo said. "Roberto, perhaps you could discover what the niece knows."

Roberto said nothing.

"It was wise of you," Eduardo said to his aunt, "to be kind to the girl this morning."

"I was sorry for her. Though I do not like the sister or the heavy-jawed brother-in-law."

She ate the last slice of *plátano*.

"Odd, isn't it," she said, "that Chilton and that other old man should die within so short a time – such bitter enemies. I suppose you, Eduardo, will attend the other's funeral on Wednesday?"

"Yes." He looked at his watch. "Roberto, you won't mind taking my class this afternoon?"

"I can't. Not today."

"What is this – mutiny?" Eduardo asked in surprise.

"No. Simply – I have something else I must do."

"But so have I. Many things. Be reasonable, *chico.*"

Teresa murmured something about mulishness and left the two brothers.

Eduardo waited for Roberto to speak. Roberto remained silent.

"Then what shall I do?"

"You could ask one of the department secretaries to give a topic for a class theme.

Also to make an assignment for the next meeting."

"I suppose so. Yes. Could you run out to the University with the topics?"

"I won't have time."

"Oh well, I'll have to do it myself." Eduardo sounded injured.

Around eleven that morning Roberto had gone to the apartment, where he found Jimmie at the telephone and Isabel and Glenn with García, Chilton's lawyer, working on papers at the table. The latter, whom Roberto knew, looked up and stretched a hand toward him. To Jimmie, when she put down the receiver, Roberto said, "I wanted to know whether I could do anything to help."

Jimmie, an unfamiliar Jimmie, ash-pale, her eyes strained, said, "Thank you, Roberto. I don't think there's anything. The telephone keeps ringing."

"It will continue to ring," García said. "I'll take the next call. The news has gone over the wire services, reached the States by now."

"You are probably too busy," Roberto said to Jimmie, "but if you felt like getting away for a few hours – I thought we might drive out to Coclé."

"An excellent idea," García said. "You

93

couldn't sleep – if you tried to rest here. Don't you agree?" He looked at Isabel and Glenn. Isabel frowned, Glenn nodded.

"The local calls will taper off," García said, "and I will be here to help with the long-distance calls. They will be heaviest later, and we can work tonight on the lists of people to be notified and other details. One thing you could do, Roberto, is to get us a pack of cable forms."

"They were going to call us," Isabel said. "The *Guardia*. But they haven't. That Captain – he said it must have been suicide. But they won't know until after –" she sobbed between a handkerchief and a bottle of smelling salts.

Jimmie spoke incisivly. "It couldn't have been suicide."

The telephone rang. García took the call.

"Well then," Roberto said, "if I come around one-thirty –"

"Please, Miss Jimmie," Victoria said, coming from the kitchen, "you go out for a little drive."

Jimmie pushed her hair back from her forehead.

"I have to get some clothes. I threw on these things. This morning."

"I could get them – from your maid?" Roberto looked at Isabel.

"No," Glenn said. "If Jimmie is determined to stay here, I will get what she needs. Now. I'll take Isabel home for a while. But I think Jimmie is out of her mind to plan to stay here alone."

"I won't be alone. Victoria is here."

García put down the receiver, made a note on a yellow pad, and said, "Mr. Furniss, there will be guards on the street. And the apartment is Jimmie's. As I told you, Mr. Chilton bought it several years ago. He told me he was deeding it to Jimmie."

"I needn't tell you – but I'll be a watch dog," Roberto said. Jimmie smiled.

"And if it isn't convenient for Mr. Furniss, I'll lend you some of my clothes."

"How would I look in watch-dog clothes?" Jimmie asked.

"Like a beautiful watch dog," García said.

Isabel looked startled, perhaps, Roberto thought, because she was unfamiliar with the ease and grace with which a Latin could deliver even an impersonal compliment.

Isabel stood up. "Let's go home, then, Glenn."

"Mr. García," Glenn said, "I'll appreciate your staying here to take calls. The charge for your time will be included in your fee."

"*María santíssima!*" García exclaimed

95

when they had gone. "Who thinks of fees? Not when such a friend –"

"You must think of fees," Jimmie said. "But my sister and her husband don't mean to be – well, mercenary. They don't –"

"They aren't used," García said, "to dealing with a Panamanian lawyer. What do they think we are? Savages without sensibilities?"

Probably yes, Roberto thought.

To his surprise, Jimmie said, "Maybe so." She placed her hand on García's. "Please thank the señora and your daughter for their messages. And thank you, señor, for all your help."

"I will see you at one-thirty," Roberto said to Jimmie. He was half-incredulous. For weeks he had longed to make an appointment with her – ever since that evening when he had met her in the campus cafe with Eduardo.

14
INTRUDER

Rain sharply stung the windshield of Roberto's car, changed to heavy washes against which the windshield wipers sloughed diligently but fallibly. Jimmie closed the windows on her side of the car.

"I don't like the wet season," she said. "And it seems so much longer than the dry season."

"Too long," Roberto said. "But usually a shower doesn't last long."

"Last night it did. It started after Uncle John went home. Oh, if only he had let me go with him – I wanted to live there. If I had been with him – maybe –"

Roberto touched her hand, the way, he thought, you touched struck-metal to still the vibrations of sound.

There was nothing to say; he thought poorly of people who attempted with banalities to stifle outbreaks of sorrow at an inexorable loss. If I had lost someone – Eduardo, Teresa – I'd be damned if I would listen to anybody that tried to keep me from

– yes, screaming. If I felt like screaming, I would scream.

In the rain the passion flowers between two walls of jungle through which the road ran glowed like blood, like fires that water would not extinguish. *Pobrecita,* he thought; (the poor little one,) erect beside him, dark glasses hiding her eyes, her face pale narrowed; but how beautiful she was, how much her beauty made him sometimes feel like singing. Never do that – it would be enough to throw her into Eduardo's arms, for Eduardo, blast him, sings very well.

The rain stopped as abruptly as it had started. In its humid wake the jungle breathed out the smell of wet fresh green growth which purified the underlying miasmic scent of airless corruption.

"Crotons," Jimmie said as they sighted an ungainly mass of the scarlet and green leaved plants whose texture reminded her of tarantula legs. "They look sinister. Why do people grow them around houses?"

"For color, I suppose. They aren't so bad here where they belong." He thought but did not tell Jimmie that crotons, separated from the jungle, took on an aggressiveness like that of the people who lived in the Canal Zone. Was much of the friction in the world due to removal from what was native – due to the

98

need for assertion against what was foreign and not understood? Too simple a theory? No generalization is true, not even this one, he remembered from reading La Rochefoucauld.

As they neared the site of the Coclé excavations, he talked to Jimmie about the Indians who had lived there and of the discoveries made by North American archaeologists on land belonging to Eduardo and himself, and on adjoining lands owned by others.

"The work wasn't finished. Surprising things turned up – columns, ruins of masonry – more sophisticated than you'd think. From all we really know about the Indians, they ran around wearing nothing but ornaments and breaking pottery utensils. Some kind of rite."

"Like breaking glasses after toasts?"

"Yes. On a pretty big scale. They did produce gold objects that they wore and put in tombs – you've probably seen some of them – *huacas*. Before the government cracked down, you could buy *huacas* cheaply enough in Panama City. And a lot of their pottery was good. They made jars and pitchers shaped like birds and animals."

"And they whistled," Jimmie said. "Uncle John had a jar shaped like a bird. When you blew into the head, the bird whistled. Eerie. Same sound the Indians heard – all those centuries back." She frowned. "He had a big heavy jaguar head – but it wasn't on the bookcase where he kept it. I noticed the empty space this morning – beside the telephone. What could have happened to it?"

"We'll try to find it."

"Roberto. This morning the police seemed to think Uncle John took his own life. I don't believe it. He had so many plans – that book he was trying to finish. Articles – lectures he was going to give in the States. And Sunday evening at Isabel's he told me he'd heard of a good man to tutor me in chemistry and was going to talk to him this week. You saw him Sunday night. Did he seem depressed?"

"No. He was very cordial – wanted to talk with me about Coclé. Asked me to stay – but I couldn't." I wish I had stayed, he thought.

"We're passing one of the sites," he said. "But you can't see anything Indian from here."

A few miles farther on he turned the car from the road and drove slowly across a stony field until they came to piles of earth and rubble.

"We won't have time to stop. I mustn't
100

keep you out too long. Over there on your left – see that fragment of a column? That's near the lower left end of the dig – it was a square. Fragments of tomb in the middle."

Near the front of the excavation he saw the wall that Chilton mentioned. It had not been there the last time Roberto had visited Coclé, a year ago, perhaps longer. A rough and unstable-looking erection, the wall surrounded a low structure only partly emerged above the earth level. A canvas covering hid whatever roofing had been laid across the tops of the walls. At the left of this building, near the surrounding wall, a shed had been built, which might have held the tools of archaeologists. Roberto saw a narrow padlocked wooden gate in the wall. Nothing was visible that might not have been related to a dig, but he knew that no authorized excavation had been done here for years.

He remembered how emphatically Eduardo had enjoined him not to come to Coclé.

And why had Chilton come here? He had been living in Panama during the period when a foundation in the United States had financed the excavations at Coclé; then would have been the time that he would have visited the site, and probably did. Had Chilton now been following the coastline in search of possible anchorages for the *Isla?* Had he been interested in the cargo that the yacht might have been carrying?

"Some day," he said to Jimmie, "when there's more time, we'll come back. And I'll show you photographs of what turned up from the dig. I have a breastplate and a golden frog."

Jimmie nodded. He saw that she was not thinking of golden frogs.

They had driven several miles back toward the city when she spoke.

"I keep thinking about that jaguar. Roberto – what if – what if Uncle John didn't drown?" Tears ran down her cheek below the sunglasses. "Nothing would be any better, either way."

Her strained control broke. She leaned against Roberto and sobbed. He skirted a sugar-cane cart drawn by two oxen, stopped the car, and put his right arm over her shoulders, and quietly held her until a larger ox-cart approached them and stopped. Jimmie moved away from him, and the dark little gnarled driver of the cart stopped to offer them sugar cane. Roberto reached across Jimmie, took the gift, and found coins for the driver.

On their return in the dusk-violet light before darkness, Roberto walked with

Jimmie to the door of the apartment building.

"There are other things I want to show you sometime – have you seen the church with the flat arch? And San José with the golden altar? It was painted black to hide the gold when the pirate Morgan came – there wasn't time to remove it."

"I'll want to see it," Jimmie said.

"You'll be all right now? I don't see the guard?"

"There's a gap sometimes when the relief comes on – there he is – it's the nice boy who carries up Victoria's market bags."

"Well then – call me if I can do anything."

Jimmie watched him cross to the door of the yellow house.

The guard coming up the hill disappeared behind the lower wall of the apartment building and came out a moment later carrying Victoria's kitten.

"Señorita, I cannot tell you how sorry I am for your loss." He gave her the kitten as if it had been an offering of flowers.

"Thank you," she said. "I wonder how the kitten got out – you haven't seen Victoria leave?"

"No," the guard said. "But those little ones are quick and sly."

103

Jimmie inserted her key in the outer door but found it unlocked, perhaps left so, she thought, by someone from one of the other apartments. On the second-floor landing the door of her uncle's apartment was not entirely closed. Calling Victoria, she entered the apartment. Against the quick-growing darkness outside, a lamp was lighted on the bookcase near the door and another light showed in the study. Beside the telephone on the bookcase lay a note from Vicky:

Miss J dear am marketing. Back soon. V.

The purring of the kitten in her arms and Victoria's note somewhat eased the chill she felt at coming into the empty apartment which would always be empty without her uncle. She stooped to set the kitten on the floor.

A sound made her look toward the study.

A man stood in the doorway.

15
GRACIELA

The door through which Jimmie had entered the apartment was only a few feet behind her. She opened it, took a step backward.

"Señorita, wait," the man said. His hand moved toward his holstered revolver as he came toward her. "I am Colonel Muñoz of the *Guardia*."

"How did you get into this apartment?"

"We have keys to all buildings with a block's radius of the *Presidencia*."

I don't believe it, Jimmie thought.

"Have you a search warrant?"

"Senorita, I do not need any authorization. In the case of such a well-known man as your uncle, certain measures must be taken."

"Like entering empty apartments – and what did you expect to find in my uncle's study?"

Jimmie's anger offset the weakness she felt in her knees. She steadied herself by placing a hand against the bookcase. The telephone – but whom could she call – and how, when this armed man stood in front of her? He was a man of medium height, heavy set, not young, not old, but his face was seamed, the skin dark, hostility and latent cruelty ran through his voice. More than that: a toad with an emanation of power, a reserve beyond whatever authority he was using here. Something he exuded challenged her fear into a surge of deeper anger.

"You have identification?" she asked.

"But naturally." He brought from a pocket a folder, which he showed her.

"Then – can't you go now? There's nothing for you to find."

He pocketed the folder. "Captain Reyes did not make a thorough investigation this morning. I am completing it. I need to know where your uncle kept his papers, the records of his researches, the manuscript for the last book that he was writing. You will tell me, señorita. At this moment."

"I can tell you nothing!"

"Come now, señorita. My request is official. Do you wish to be arrested for withholding evidence?"

"Evidence of what? Was it a crime – of my uncle's – that he died this morning? Or was murdered? Is it a crime of mine – that I don't know where his papers are?"

She turned, took the telephone directory from a shelf in the bookcase.

"You are not to use the telephone."

"I will use it – to call the United States Embassy."

The Colonel grasped her wrists. The telephone directory fell to the floor. He spoke quietly, but currents of hostility and latent cruelty ran through his voice.

"Listen to me. If it would make you more reasonable – you would be

106

paid for delivering the papers to us."

"Take your hands off me!" Jimmie cried.

If she screamed, she thought, who would come? The boy at the door – a subordinate of the toad-colonel?

Muñoz released her.

"Certainly," he said. "It is no pleasure to me to hold you. But –"

Footsteps sounded on the stairway, and the telephone rang.

Jimmie turned to face the open door. Muñoz seized the receiver and answered.

Insteady of Vicky, whom she she expected, Jimmie saw Graciela García, the lawyer's daughter and her closest friend.

"Jimmie!" Graciela embraced her, then, seeing Muñoz, dropped her arms.

Jimmie tried to snatch the telephone receiver from Muñoz, but he held it high and pushed her away.

"Yes, I understand who you are señor. The publisher...A tragic occurrence. And one that must deeply concern you...Ah, yes, the manuscript. It must be impounded here during the investigation. Do you have a copy of any parts of it?...No? Well, we will have to notify you later...Who am I? I am Colonel Muñoz of the *Guardia Nacional*... No, señor, the niece is unavailable at this moment."

107

Jimmie leaned over him, shouted into the telephone. "I am not unavailable – I –"

Again Muñor pushed her away. "Of course we will communicate with you... Good-by, señor."

More footsteps sounded on the stairs. Victoria appeared at the door; behind her the young guard carried her shopping bag.

"Miss Jimmie," Vicky said. "I thought you might eat lamb chops –" she halted, seeing the Colonel and Graciela.

"Return to your post," the Colonel ordered the guard. "And you –" he faced Jimmie. "Eat your chops." He did not need to add "and choke on them." His meaning was clear. He stalked out of the apartment.

Jimmie sank into the chair at the table.

"Brandy, Vicky – she is so pale!" Graciela cried.

"No – I must call the Embassy!" Jimmie cried.

An aide to the Ambassador was polite, friendly, but not helpful. She was, he reminded her, in a foreign country; the investigation seemed to be necessary. Yes, he would give His Excellency the message but there was, he thought, nothing that could be done at that end. He regretted deeply what had happened to John Chilton. The conversation was a brush-off, Jimmie realized: the Embassy at this critical stage of the second treaty's consideration wanted no complication.

"My father will be here soon," Graciela said. "He will know what to do."

"You're both mighty pale," Vicky said. "No wonder. I've seen that man before. Once I worked for a judge and his family, and that man used to come to the house. I saw him kick the judge's pregnant dog – he thought he was alone in the room."

Jimmie shivered. Graciela put an arm around her.

The two girls were the same age, both had shell-pale skin. Jimmie was a little taller and thinner, her eyes violet-blue, her hair bronze-chestnut; Graciela's eyes and hair were Spanish jet-black. A strong friendship linked the two.

Vicky brought brandy. The kitten jumped into Jimmie's lap as she sat at the table.

"I tried to call you, Jimmie, as soon as I got your message. My mother and I had been shopping – hoping you might come to stay with us. You know how we felt about your uncle. How we would want you to be with us."

"Thank you, Graci. But I want to stay here. I can't understand – about that message. I didn't call you."

"A maid took the message – said a man had called. I thought it might have been your brother-in-law."

"No," Jimmie said. "I don't know who it could have been. But I'm glad you're here, Graci. Stay if you can – for dinner?"

"I must go now, to be with my mother, who is much distressed by what has happened. My father will be here soon."

"Your father," Jimmie said, "is an enormous help." But, she thought, who could help, whom could she appeal to, if the *Guardia* were poised like vultures – vultures with keys – for a descent at any moment? Roberto. The thought of Roberto warmed her more than the brandy.

And tomorrow her uncle's papers would be destroyed. When he had spoken to her of these papers in the vault, she had only half-listened; for on that evening, months ago, his life had been vigorous and dependable. She had not realized that he had been planning for the disposition of his papers in the case of his death.

16
EMERGENCY FOR
THE CONDOR

The two men were meeting for the first time in the place they had planned to use when an emergency required an immediate conference. Although this place was more comfortable than their regular headquarters, particularly today when the heaviest rain of the newly arrived wet season was falling, it lacked the security of the other place, also the secretiveness and the austerity which intensified their feeling of dedication to their purposes.

Ostensibly the two were meeting to plan the memorial ceremony for their old associate who had died in the hospital; there was no secret about their past acquaintance, apart from the deeper and secret relationship that they had formed.

"I thought," the younger man said brusquely, "that we had agreed not to take unilateral action."

"The same thought occurred to me," the other said. "Ah well, let us accept what God has sent and ask each other no questions."

"If we had to depend on God – well, you can have your God-guided routine. We have a problem that needs our action at once. Our new partner is a very shrewd man. Within a few hours of that drowning in the marina, he put together some things he heard and others that he guessed. What he said convinced me that those famous papers are going to be destroyed immediately."

The other man frowned. "That must not happen. We need those papers. Together with the files of our late partner – which luckily we *do* have – the total would be a strong resource. The lawyer, I suppose, has the papers or access to them?"

"Our young friend and new associate thinks so."

"They couldn't be in worse hands. From our point of view. Except perhaps in the hands of that newspaper editor. And how do we know – even if the lawyer carries out a direction to destroy them – that he will not keep some of them for his own use?"

"We don't know."

The older man bent his long bony fingers into a fist and pounded his desk.

"We must act immediately. The owner of those papers – records – perhaps diaries – was reported to have amassed voluminous materials. He had a kind of puritanical – even fanatical – obsession with factual proof. Someone else, less rigid, could damage our plans. I give you one example: I believe this old North American, the investigator, made contact with the widow of a man who endangered us and had to be removed. You will remember the case. A chauffeur managed to overhear conversations between our dead colleague and one of your subordinates concerning a legislator, a so-called liberal, who was gaining too much support. Measures were to be taken. The chauffeur was in a position to blackmail us."

"I remember the case," the younger man said. "The old man bungled it. He lived too long."

"Possibly. The chauffeur's widow and children live in another country. They were provided for. But the North American visited the town where they live. However, don't be too ready to condemn our old colleague. He had a wide following. Much influence. A spellbinder whom many of the poor and ignorant seemed to love. You will admit that you and I, though more intelligent, more cautious, have no qualities that would endear us to the masses."

"Let's hope our new colleague can supply
113

that deficiency," the younger man said acidly.

"How did he learn of the planned destruction of the North American's papers?"

"He went to the apartment early this morning to make a sympathy call. You know he found the body around three-thirty in the night?"

"Yes, from a news program at seven this morning."

"You get up early."

"I have early duties. So – what happened at the apartment?"

"The nieces, the husband of one niece, the lawyer were there. The atmosphere suggested a disagreement. While the maid was letting our friend enter, he caught a few words – something about a memorandum and the destruction of files. The married niece was hostile toward the lawyer. That was enough. I told you the boy is very shrewd. You were right about his intelligence."

"Yes. But – did he tell you these things over the telephone?"

"Don't worry. He is as good as we are about disguising information."

"When will he return?"

"Late tonight. He is to be interrogated by Captain Reyes this afternoon, then will drive to the ship."

"Reyes." The older man frowned. "Why Reyes?"

"Because he was on duty last night. I would not have chosen him. But I cannot be on duty twenty-four hours a day. I agree with you about Reyes. I do not trust a man whom I cannot buy."

"Of all the members of your forces, Reyes is the most recalcitrant. Ah well, we can outthink him. So now – we have first to contain the lawyer. Then, I think, block whatever the editor of the newspaper might do. He must be stopped. The paper halted. We will not permit a martyrization in the death of the North American." The older man lifted a thin wooden kris from Bali which he used as a paper knife, examined it as though he had not seen it before.

The telephone on the dark massive Spanish desk rang, and the older man answered, at first suavely; then his voice became authoritative. "By no means...no. Impossible. Not for a non-believer...no, not even a prayer. You will excuse me now – I have duties." He replaced the receiver.

"Effrontery!" he exclaimed. "The North American had wanted a prayer – in case of death – by one of our priests. A man whom we cannot have here in the city."

115

"Wouldn't it be simpler to let the priest mumble a few words – than to risk hostility?"

"Too late for that. He's already hostile."

He glanced at the desk clock. "I have duties – quickly, then. Offer to buy the papers."

"That has been done. No success."

"Then exert pressure on the lawyer. Can he be bought?"

"No," the younger man said bluntly.

"He has a daughter."

"You mean a kidnaping? A ransom demand?" The younger man scowled. "I do not like warring on women."

"What better leverage?" his colleague asked.

"If it had to be done – there is the other girl. The niece."

The older man shook his head. "No. For her return, there would be lacking the force of parental anxiety."

The other man, still frowning, touched against his cheek the cold jade stone in a ring he wore. "I suppose I will have to implement your plan. But where do we – entertain our – guest?"

"You will, I am sure, think of suitable arrangements – a place that is secure – a woman to care for a possibly drugged girl.

116

Ransom calls to the father." He added, "Do not forget that the newspaper editor must also be controlled. Immediately. And we will meet in our usual place tomorrow or possibly Wednesday to confirm our plans for action after the second Canal Treaty vote. The posters have been prepared – with sufficient ambiguity to fit either outcome?"

"Yes."

The older man rose, gaunt, tall.

"Before you go," the other man said, "I have a suggestion in case we need an incident to bring the hostility in the Zone to the boil. There are, as you know, two North American cemeteries here, one on the Pacific side, the other near the Atlantic end of the Canal. A little desecration of tombs –"

The sallow face of his companion paled. He opened a desk drawer, took out a bottle of pills, poured water from a jug on his desk, and swallowed a pill. A church bell sounded.

"No," he said. "The dead do not shoot."

17
THE ISLA'S CARGO

At some other time, Eduardo thought, I could like this clear-eyed, quiet-mannered Captain Reyes of the Guardia Nacional.

They met in the library of the yellow house. Eduardo noticed Reyes's appreciative glances at the ceiling-high bookcases of leather-bound books.

It was Monday afternoon of the same day on which John Chilton's body had been brought from the marina. Eduardo had scarcely had time to telephone the University to instruct the secretary who would give assignments to his class.

Ahmad, the Japanese houseboy, served coffee. Where, Eduardo thought, have you been resurrected from? Paula had been carrying on Ahmad's duties for two days. Well, no matter. Over coffee, he repeated what he had told Reyes in the early morning. But the Captain went farther now, questioning Eduardo about the time at which he had observed the body in the marina and whether the other members of his family had seen it.

"The time – oh, two-thirty – approximately. And my aunt and brother did not see the body. They were about to go to bed when I saw it."

"About to?" Reyes repeated. "How long an interval?"

"A few minutes," Eduardo answered.

"You waited during those minutes – they might have been important."

"More coffee, Captain?"

"No thank you." Reyes made a note in the notebook on the arm of his chair. "You told me this morning that the body seemed to have been caught on a mooring line of one of the yachts. Which yacht was it?"

"I don't remember. The sight was – too horrible."

"Your yacht, the *Isla Amarilla,* was moored in the marina yesterday, I believe. She wasn't there this morning. When did she sail?"

"I don't know. Sometime during the night. She is under charter to a fisherman."

"Why did she come into the marina?" Reyes asked.

"For minor repairs."

"Had the repairs been made?"

"I imagine so. I'll know when I get the bill."

"Why would the charterer sail at night or in the early morning?"

Eduardo shrugged. "Fishermen are unpredictable

"Who is the charterer?"

"His name is Miguel Martín."

"You have a written charter agreement?"

"No – our arrangements were verbal. I've done business with Miguel for years."

"He is Panamanian?"

"No. A Texan."

"Do you know where Martín and your yacht could be reached?"

"No," Eduardo answered. "He doesn't consult with me about his choice of fishing grounds. I am no fisherman, Captain."

"Does he employ a crew?"

"His wife. And he may have picked up other hands."

"The *Isla* had sailed when you brought John Chilton's body toward the shore?"

"Yes.

You didn't see her sail?"

"It was late – early morning – when I came home. I did not notice – or look for the *Isla*." I must, he thought, warn Teresa and Roberto to forget what was said about the ship, about a possible cruise.

Reyes's next shot came close.

"You have heard of El Condor, señor?"

120

"Who hasn't?" Eduardo said easily.

"Do you know of any connection between the Condor and señor Chilton?"

"But I thought the opinion this morning was that Chilton had committed suicide. Has there been a different verdict?"

"You didn't answer my question, señor."

"My answer would be no," Eduardo said. "But surely the *Guardia* would know more about the Condor –"

"We are investigating thoroughly," Reyes said. "I shall want to talk again with your aunt and your brother. Are they here now?"

"Unfortunately no. My brother, I know, went briefly to see señor Chilton Sunday night. Were other visitors observed?"

"Two other visitors. The first, a man whom the guard did not recognize, stayed probably an hour. At most, two hours. On leaving, he waved to señor Chilton, whom the guard saw sitting at a desk inside a window facing the street. The second – the guard thinks he was a United States soldier, remained a shorter time. When he left, señor Chilton was still at the desk inside the window."

The interview with Reyes delayed Eduardo past the time he had hoped to set out to find the *Isla.* He drove more cautiously than usual. It would be awkward today to be halted by traffic police. Behind him he left the city's tall white buildings and in crossing the Bridge of the Americas high above the Canal, slowed to a stop so that he could look out at the slender long peninsula of Amador pointed into the Pacific and fringed by goldshot royal palms. Beyond Amador small islands were smoke-blue. Inland, to the right, the cresting range of the Cordillera seemed to flow, tenuous, through pools of violet-blue shadow.

Below the bridge and to the left, in the slash that cut the thin throat of the Isthmus, a freighter with a red, white and blue funnel and the flag of the United States moved into the Pacific. A passenger ship showing the green of the Italian Line followed. In the Balboa anchorage other ships were waiting until the next morning to transit the Canal to the Caribbean. Eduardo started his car and headed toward the sundered interior of his country.

Before he reached Arraijan, the first town beyond the bridge, beyond the Zone, a shower started. Between towns, in little adobe or wattle huts with peaked thatch roofs, candlelight and lamplight showed. The headlights picked out green waving banana leaves, red berries on coffee trees, two thin dun-colored dogs running homeward. He smelled wood fires mingled with onion and garlic. By the time he reached Chorrera the rain had stopped and the air had what he thought was a peculiarly Panamanian smell of freshly moistened green growths and flowers. Once he had wanted to write a novel about Panama. He gripped the wheel and whistled to bring himself out of a useless despondency.

And you, Roberto, he thought, whom we impose on because you are young and too fond of our aunt and of me, you will, you must stay free from – he didn't want to think the word but felt it forming in his throat muscles – the word *depravity*. He saw in his mind Roberto's face, the carved-ivory fineness of bone, the hauteur of feature which through centuries had distinguished Villalba faces; their aunt Teresa might have been a twin sister of the Villalba beauty who had married a Viceroy in the early seventeenth century. In Roberto's face the heritage of arrogance had not appeared. Along with the ancestral purposiveness and vigor, Roberto showed something not visible in the portraits – what was it? A readiness to halt in judging? A clear and independent habit of reasoning despite pressures from the narrow-channeled wills of the people who tried to dominate him? Eduardo thought of these pressures, of his own, at least, not so much in exculpation as in explanation. Villalbas at his age had recognized their responsibility in dominating wives and children. Am I, he thought, substituting Roberto for the family members that I do not have?

He groped for solace in looking toward no matter how ephemeral a reunion with Rita.

Are all like this, he wondered, all of us Panamanians who manage to keep our heads above the crowd, manage to go to a university because of our family's tradition or resources – do we either yield to indolence or find ourselves caught up in vitiating, extraneous involvements?

The drive was giving him an escape from immediate troubling action but not from its pursuit in his mind. Now that he was working with the men whom earlier he had worked for indirectly, he had become convinced that they were madmen, crazed in their campaign for power and irrational in their methods of securing it. The old man whose place he had taken, as a third in the group but junior to the other two, had repeated, if brief, attainments of political power to explain his addiction to conspiracy. But the other two, the priest and the soldier, seemed demented children ready to burn a

124

building for the sake of a few candies buried in the rubble. For if these men succeeded in destroying the fragile stability of Panama and in emerging as its rulers, they would find themselves in command of a ghost country, bloodless and hopeless. Or be caught themselves in the avalanche of destruction. The old politician who had just died had at least held to the concept of Panama as an entity. He had been a despot, not a gambler with devastation. But in meeting with the remaining two members of El Condor, Eduardo had been appalled at the plans they bandied back and forth, as if each was trying to outdo the other: the idea that they might sabotage the Canal, whichever way the vote went in the United States Senate on the second of the treaties; the suggestion of assassinating the President of the United States if he came to Panama with the instruments of ratification; an assault on the Canal Zone – these ideas thrown out casually – by citizens of a country without an army.

And the two men who handled the dynamite of these ideas as if they were ivory chessmen – these were the men he was committed to work with, had worked for, indirectly for several years. How had it started? His need for money? Ambition? I was a miserable guilty fool, he thought, when

I leased the *Isla* for smuggling arms to a Condor agent, when I let them store the arms, have their meetings at Coclé. Even then I guessed at their identity but was not sure. The agent, two or three grades below the top men, claimed not to know who they were.

The quick, punctual darkness had fallen when he came to Anton. Here he left the highway and drove toward the ocean over a rutted road through banana plantations, past an abandoned sugar mill, into an even more rudimentary track which ended at the shore. The darkness over the ocean was misted, pointed with starlight in the bone-white foam.

He drove along the beach to a grove of mangoes and palms where he could hide the car. From here he used a flashlight to find and follow a familiar trail through a strip of jungle. Ahead he heard the soft surge of waves. Then, stopping to brush away an insect, he heard a nearer sound on his right: a footstep crunching on a rotted log.

"Who is there?" he called, turning the flash beam toward the sound. He caught sight of a figure slowly moving away from him. Leaving the trail, he ran to the right, but before he overtook the man, the flashlight showed only matted vines and tree

126

trunks although Eduardo still heard footsteps. He started to call again; but his cry was
choked by a slicing blow from the edge of a
flattened hand. As he fell, another sharp
blow struck his head. Consciousness drained
from him.

"Eduardo!"

He became aware of Rita's voice and in the
light from her flash saw her bending over
him. Miguel stood beside her. Eduardo
pulled himself to his feet.

"Who was that man?"

"Come on board," Rita said, grasping his
arm. "Miguel, take his other arm."

On board the *Isla*, she brought coffee to
Eduardo, who sat on the edge of a bunk,
testing with his fingers the bruises on his
throat.

"Are these marks going to show, *chica?*"
he asked.

"Probably. You must wear a scarf. And
I will put a piece of steak on your eye."

"No. If I have to, I'll wear a patch. No
meat."

"We knew you would come, Eduardo,"
Rita said with unusual warmth. "Miguel saw
you take the body toward the shore last night
– then the lights, the *policia*. We listened
to the radio. Did Chilton threaten us
immediately?"

"He could have threatened any number of people," Eduardo answered wearily.

"Was his death – well, hastened by our revered leaders?"

"The police seem to think it was suicide. But tell me about the man who attacked me."

"We did not act wisely." Rita's words were apologetic, but her tone defiant. "Well, would you have had us let the man drown? Are we so hard pressed – yet? So we took him on board. We were coming around the point below your house. It was not yet day. A shout. There was a man in the water calling for help. Miserably. And probably fraudulently, for when he escaped just now, he swam ashore. But then we took him on board. He said his name was Smith. An American. Then – what to do with him?"

"What did you do?"

"Locked him in a cabin. Covered the window from outside. Miguel went ashore to telephone, and the truck came very soon. We unloaded the cases, and put them into the truck. Just before dark. Miguel and I were ashore with the truck driver – I happened to look back at the ship – and saw the man Smith's face at the window. He had managed to break the cover. Then everything happened at once. Before Miguel and I could

128

get back on board, darkness came and the man battered down the cabin door, jumped in the water. We got flashlights and hunted for him. Once we saw him at the edge of the jungle limping. But before we caught him, he hid. We were still hunting for him when you came."

"Did he see the cases of guns?" Eduardo asked.

Rita shrugged. "Unless he was blind."

"He limped, you say?"

"Badly."

"He may have hurt his foot coming ashore," Eduardo said.

"Or landed on a snake or a scorpion."

"Was he armed?"

"No," Rita said. "He wore khaki trousers and an undershirt. Nothing in his pockets but some coins tied up in a handkerchief."

"You took the coins?"

"No. We are not paid for piracy."

"Pardon me," Eduardo said with sarcasm. He added more seriously, "Why the devil did he jump me – why not just keep running?"

"Because he probably couldn't run. And you were closing in on him." She added unhappily, "He didn't have shoes."

"No shoes – and in the jungle all night! God! Couldn't you have put him ashore somewhere?"

"And have him go running around talking about the *Isla?* Remember – we didn't plan to have him run into the jungle. I tell you, Eduardo – we fed him. I hoped we could ditch him in Cuba. He must have been strong as an ox."

"He was," Eduardo said, fingers on throat. "He couldn't have been investigating the *Isla* – not a North American, not in such an obvious risky way. So he must have been running away from something. Some crime in Panama? Or – suppose he was a deserter from an Army base in the Zone – his trousers – did they look part of a uniform? His haircut?"

"Perhaps," Rita said. "I remember now – he wore a kind of wristband. Maybe with identification. We were too busy to examine it – we were trying to take as many cases as we could ashore, to save time when the truck came. Well, your eminence, what do we do next?"

She will never love me, Eduardo thought, stung by the sharpness of her voice. He tried to shake off his distress at the thought of the boy wandering, shoeless, injured in the jungle at night – a distress deeper than his worry about what the boy had seen, about what he might report concerning the *Isla*'s cargo.

"First," he said, covering his trouble with firmness, 'we cannot hunt for the boy in the jungle at night. Second, you and Miguel must go back as soon as possible to Cuba. Start tonight. Get the repairs finished there, bring another cargo back here."

"Start tonight?" Rita said. "You aren't staying?"

No invitation, no regret; only the need to have the instructions clear.

He set the coffee cup on a table beside the bunk and drew Rita toward him.

"I am staying for one hour," he said.

Unsmiling, her gypsy face dark under heavy eyebrows, she let him remove her blue shorts and shirt, trace the tan of her body around the paler contours of what had been covered by bikinis, stretch her out on the bunk underneath him.

Who, what are you? he thought, pressing his lips against her lean tanned body, outlining with his hands the paler areas. You have told me that you were Portuguese, or Brazilian, once a flamenco dancer, a courier for revolutionists in North Africa – you pose as Miguel's wife but aren't – I know only that you are a damascened blade, cold to touch, but lambent underneath from the firing of the steel.

18
DEATH OF A NEWSPAPER

After leaving Jimmie on Monday around six, Roberto crossed the paved parking area and semicourt, lined with oleanders, hibiscus, and tree-sized blooming poinsettias, and entered the main door of the yellow house. The side of the house facing the street was windowless and doorless; no wonder people have trouble finding a way in, he thought, but he liked the faceless fronts of Spanish houses.

Eduardo and Teresa were out. In the kitchen Paula was preparing a fish for his dinner.

"Just keep the fish warm somewhere – then you can leave," he told Paula. "Where are Ahmad and Maria?"

"Where they usually are – out," Paula answered good-naturedly. "I'm sorry about Mr. Chilton," she added. "I made some rolls and a chocolate cake and took it over there – I hope that was all right?"

"Very good. Thank you, Paula."

He spent most of an hour finishing an

article for Ahora, then telephoned the offices, expecting to find San Martín, the owner and editor, still at work as usual, but no one answered. A second call, to his friend's house, brought a response in an unfamiliarly grave voice.

"What is wrong?" Roberto asked quickly.

"Everything. They have us, Roberto. My offices are shut down. Mortgage foreclosure. I was a week behind in payments – but that has happened before. I was served with eviction papers."

"Then can't you do the editing – the makeup – somewhere else? Here, for example?"

"No good. The printer has broken his contract. He says his union pressmen will strike rather than print Ahora. God knows I am not anti-union, but when I see corruption I report it. Sorry about your article, *amigo*. That is the one on urging moderation, patience about the Canal Treaties."

"Yes," Roberto said. "I've just finished it. I wish I could do something about all this."

"I don't know what anyone can do. Everything came at once – Chilton's murder. Roberto, he was one of my dearest friends.

He and García. We were planning an article – a kind of follow-up to yours. In some ways he was the clearest voice speaking for liberal forces in Panama. The best journalist I have ever known. And the warmest of friends. If the medical examiners call his death suicide – I'll have to publish. Somehow."

"A Xerox sheet?"

"How to distribute? The newsdealers are unionized. They will adopt whatever stand the pressmen take."

"We'll deliver the sheets ourselves," Roberto said. "You, I – and some of my friends at the University. What about radio time – television?"

"And how pay? I can't. You know how close we ran to the ground."

"I know you always paid me."

"All I could. Little enough. And listen, Roberto – this morning I called the offices of the Governor of the Canal Zone – talked with an aide – somebody named Austin. Do you know what effrontery he had? Chilton, he said, had undoubtedly taken his own life – he had made so many enemies with his wild radicalism. The ghoul sounded happy – ay, *demonio*, happy about the murder. And now I can't even find out what the United States media are reporting – not without my teletype."

"Can García help you?"

"Whoever has ruined me will be gunning for García too. We had leads – Chilton and García and I – leads to the virus here – to the Condor."

"I will see what I can do about the Xeroxing," Roberto said. "Don't give up. How is your wife?"

"Valiant and beautiful."

"Thanks to God for that."

"And keep your article, Roberto. Keep it safe. I could pay you something –"

"No, no," Roberto said.

He forgot to eat Paula's fish until it had become a blackened skeleton.

19
ABDUCTION

Jimmie would have liked to forget that Monday night's meeting at which she and García found Glenn and Isabel in disagreement with them in every attempt that they made to comply with what they knew to be Chilton's wishes.

Isabel looked ill; Glenn showed nothing of his usual bland composure. Patiently

García – Jimmie marvelled at his tolerance – explained the procedures he would follow. The police by now had released Chilton's body for burial. García, who had tried to reach them earlier by telephone, had made arrangements with a funeral home for a brief prayer and then burial in a Protestant cemetery in Panama City on Wednesday.

"Impossible!" Glenn exclaimed. "He will be buried in the cemetery at this end of the Zone. And services will be held by our minister."

"Glenn," Jimmie interposed, "he wouldn't have wanted that. Panama was his home. Señor García knows – Uncle John did not want a funeral – only a prayer by his friend, Father Luis."

"Your uncle isn't here now to dictate what he wants," Glenn said cruelly. "He will not be buried in Panama."

"That, I think," García said, "brings us to the subject we touched on this morning. The paper from your uncle instructing me to destroy immediately all his files. His papers, notebooks, microfilms."

"I believe that is illegal," Glenn said. "The papers are part of the estate. The executor –"

"Glenn," Jimmie said. "Señor García is the executor."

"A foreigner?" Glenn got up and walked to the balcony door.

"Your wife's uncle," García said quietly, "was a resident of a foreign country. And I regard the memorandum, which was witnessed and signed, as a legal instrument."

Glenn turned back from the terrace door. "The papers are valuable. Like any other part of the inheritance. The book that he was writing – what about that?"

"It will not be finished," García said.

"Not finished – not published?" Isabel cried. "But we will start a suit – if you go ahead with this."

"You would have difficulties, señora," García said. "Do you speak Spanish?"

"Why should I speak Spanish?"

"You would need interpreters at every point," García said.

"I talked with the Governor today – and God knows he had more urgent matters to deal with."

How can they haggle, Jimmie thought? Why do they seem more disturbed now than by first knowledge of our loss of Uncle John?

"Mr. Furniss," García said quietly, "I can understand how you feel. But I know what my client's wishes were. And I am bound to carry them out. Also, by now – I could not

137

reach you earlier – your uncle's body will have been transferred to the funeral home here. There has been no public announcement, but an inquest has confirmed what we guessed – that your uncle was murdered. There was a heavy blow – struck on his head – before immersion in the marina."

"So now we have two cemeteries claiming the body," Glenn said. "As if it were a trophy! Your client, García, was a renegade."

"Please, Glenn," Isabel said. "Please. He was my uncle. I know you have had a terrible day – not only this – and I know that Clay thinks Uncle John's papers should be destroyed –"

"Interpreters? But *why* – can't these people speak English?"

"Isabel," Jimmie said. "Cool it. Come back to the main point. What Uncle John wanted."

"I will not! We will sue."

"The only grounds," García said, "that I can think of would be mental incompetence or undue influence."

"No. He was not incompetent – and Jimmie – no undue influence," Isabel wept. "Not Jimmie. What would she get out of it?"

"Isabel," Glenn ordered. "We will go home."

"Yes, Vicky," Jimmie said when her sister and brother-in-law had gone. "Now please bring us Scotch." To García she said, "Señor, I am sorry. About it all."

"These things are minor, Jimmie, compared with our loss."

When the telephone rang at ten-fifteen, Victoria answered.

"For you, señor," she said to García.

"No, she had left before I came . . . not yet? A moment." He turned to Jimmie: "Did Graci say she was going anywhere on her way home?"

"No – she said she was going directly home. She left around seven-thirty."

He spoke again to his wife on the telephone: "She was going home from here . . . What! . . . . What did the man say? . . . an exchange? My God! You aren't alone? . . . tell the maids not to let anyone enter. I will be with you as soon as possible."

"Almost three hours ago she left here," he said to Jimmie. "She has not arrived. And my wife has just had a telephone call from a man who said he had a message for me – about an exchange – for my daughter."

When he had left, Jimmie and Victoria faced each other bleakly, without words.

139

20
THE OXCART

I will go anyway, Father Luis thought. If I cannot go as an officiating priest, I will go as a civilian. But I will not fail John Chilton.

The neighbor who occasionally cooked for him had left stewed chicken and breadfruit for his dinner. He gave a generous serving to Negrito, his cat.

"Never reproach me again, Negrito, for skimping your meals."

Negrito, he could have sworn, looked at him with concern, and was slow to enjoy the feast.

He spent some time praying for the soul of his friend and for the strength to comprehend and make conciliation with the actions of his superiors. At the end of that time he tried, as he had tried several times before, to reach Chilton's niece by telephone. The time was now almost eleven. The line was still busy.

Pobrecita, he thought. I must call her in the morning. He opened the door to let Negrito go out. A late-rising moon silvered the tower of the church. The scent of flowers and flowering trees in the little plaza filled the two rooms of his house. At night the past seemed near: he felt close to the valiance and persistence of the priests who had accompanied the conquistadores and had battled bloodlessly against their savagery.

He read for an hour and was preparing to go to bed when he heard the wooden groan and creak of an oxcart's wheels. The driver called to his oxen; the cart stopped in front of the priest's cottage.

"*Padre* – are you there?"

"I am here. Do you need help?" It was not new for Father Luis to be called on for help by people in this area of few priests and fewer doctors. He was accustomed to giving whatever medical aid he could to the ill or injured, and to trying, when necessary, to send them to the nearest hospital.

"Who is hurt? You, my son?"

"No, *padre*. I found this boy wandering around – out of his mind. Near the sugar mill. Bitten by some insect." The driver named a village over ten miles away.

"Help me bring him inside." Together they carried the boy into the cottage, to the priest's bed.

"He has a wrist band," the oxcart driver said. "A North American soldier?"

141

Father Luis brought the lamp nearer and read the named Clifford Hanley and the designation of the Army unit to which the soldier was – had been? – attached.

After sponging the sunburned feverish face, the priest laid a wet cloth over the boy's forehead.

"What is your name, my son?" he asked the driver.

"Juan Gómez, *padre.*"

"You made a long trip to bring this poor boy here, Juan."

"The oxen made the trip."

"And would be grateful for water – and you, too. Here is a pail and a cup. The well is behind the house."

"There is something in the boy's pocket, *padre.*"

"*Pobrecito* – he is not even wearing shoes, only some palm leaves twisted around his feet."

Hanley wore a mud-stained undershirt and khaki trousers with a pocket, from which the priest took a handkerchief knotted around a handful of gold coins: ancient Spanish coins.

Could they be – it was unlikely – but still – could they be coins from John Chilton's collection? He frowned.

"We will keep them safe," he told Juan,

142

who was staring at the coins in amazement. "Go to the well now, and then you shall have food."

When Juan came back, the priest gave him the rest of the chicken, with bread and cheese and red wine. Juan grunted with satisfaction as he ate. "A demon of a hunger I had, *Padre.*"

"I hope the oxen will find some grass around the house."

"Pedro and Pablo will find grass anywhere. They never complain. They are beasts to deserve your blessing, *Padre.*"

"They shall have it," the priest said, wishing that he had grain as well as blessings to give the faithful animals. He had always had a warm feeling for oxen. With faint nostalgia for legends, he wondered whether midnight should be the time for the blessing. Negrito, he thought, should share; but he knew that Negrito would more enjoy a freshly caught mouse.

"That boy," Juan said, "kept mumbling about a boat, about guns, about something that sounded like *empi.*"

"Military Police," the priest said, "I fear he is a deserter. Did he say anything more about the guns?"

"Many guns. He sounded very unhappy. You can cure him?"

143

"I will try, Juan. And you must rest here tonight. I have no other bed, but there are blankets."

"Thank you, *Padre*. I will unharness the animals and then sleep in the cart. The boy?"

"He is still unconscious. His left leg is badly swollen, from an insect bite, as you said."

An hour later, when Juan was sleeping in the cart, and Negrito had returned for his night ration of canned milk, Father Luis sat beside the bed. And soon, after he had replaced for the third time the wet cloth on the boy's forehead, and applied an antiseptic to the leg, he saw the boy's eyes open. It was a crucial moment: what would the eyes show – memory of a crime – or merely the clouded awakening to consciousness? The eyes were a lucid blue. They met the priest's, and the boy put out his hand. The priest took it. He did not believe in the validity of instant judgment but was moved by the childlike candor of those eyes.

He brought wine, raised the boy's head, and held the cup to his lips.

"That is good. Now you shall have soup."

He warmed a can of chicken broth. Unaided, Hanley drank it from a cup.

"You are feeling better?"

"Yes. Where am I?"

"You are safe here, in Natá. I am Father Luis."

Hanley made a sound like laughter.

"I thought I was dying, Father. Would have saved a lot of trouble."

"Your coins are safe. In the morning you will tell me how you got them. Lie still now. I must put more medicine on your leg. Painful, no?"

"Hurts like hell. But I can tell you, *padre*, all this feels great. How did I get here?"

"The driver of an oxcart found you – brought you here. Over ten miles."

"My God! *Padre* – if he's still here – give him some of the coins, will you? I didn't really want to be kept alive, but that man didn't know."

"I can't give him any of the coins. Not until you tell me how you got them. Can you remember?"

Hanley closed his eyes. "I remember. But I don't want to."

"Sleep, then. Your belt is tight – shall I remove it?"

"No, no!" Hanley clutched the twisted snakeskin. As if the dank whiplike belt had emitted poison, his face became more flushed and he mumbled words in delirium. He raised himself from the pillow, now seemed to be ejecting words as though freeing himself from a painful accretion. Father Luis thought of the green stain forming in kerosene in which a snake-poisoned arm or leg had been soaked. As he listened, he felt compunction. He was hearing an involuntary confession, and he feared that the boy would tell him of involvement in a crime. But he must listen – he would deal with the necessities of disclosure later – he must ask questions, which even in delirium the boy answered almost gratefully.

There had been a crime, yes. But the boy had not commited it, only concealed it. And he had taken some of John Chilton's coins from the box on the desk.

"His head – oh God, he had been killed horribly – then strapped into that chair by the window – where the police guard would see him – to confuse them about the time. If there had been anything I could do – but there wasn't. And who would have believed I didn't do it? Only, I have the belt. Not Chilton's. He wouldn't have worn anything like that. And he wouldn't have minded about the coins. He was my friend."

The boy was at the threshold of consciousness, the delirium fading. Negrito,

146

on the priest's knees, put out a paw and touched Cliff's arm.

"Tell me – he wouldn't have minded, would he?"

"No, I don't think so. Now tell *me* – did you know that señor Chilton's body was found in the marina?"

"No. But the murderer must have come back – there are vines up and down over the balconies at the back –"

The boy put his hand over Negrito's paw. "I have a cat. At home."

"Where is your home, my son?"

"South Dakota – you know where that is? Will I ever be able to go there?" He gathered Negrito into his arms.

"I know where South Dakota is. And I will try to help you go there. But you have deserted from the Army?"

"Yes. Mr. Chilton tried to keep me from doing it – but maybe he would have helped me. He could do anything, *Padre*, why did it have to happen?"

"Why indeed," the priest said. He brought a cup of milk. "Drink this."

Juan Gómez, rubbing his eyes, came to the front door.

"*Padre* – the blessing – for the oxen?"

It was midnight. Father Luis took Negrito and went out into the flower-spiced night, to the dim bulks of the oxen behind the cottage. An anachronism, he thought, as he delivered a brief blessing for the oxen and for Negrito; but not without comfort even to a priest who read proscribed books and was censured by his superiors. One of the oxen spoke gently.

"Which one was that, Juan?"

"Pedro. He thanks you, *Padre.*"

When he came back to Cliff, Father Luis found the boy sitting up.

"I thought you had gone away."

"No. Only blessing the animals. Here is Negrito to sleep beside you. I think you will want to tell me something else. How you came up the coast."

Hanley told him.

"They kept you locked in the cabin – and you saw the cases – did you see guns?"

"No. But the cases were the right size. What else could they hold? And there were boxes of ammunition."

"They were loaded into the truck?"

"Yes. The two people on the boat and the truck driver – loaded them."

"Did you see the name of the boat?"

"Yes – when I got away – *Isla* – something else. Spanish." Cliff laughed. "I was in jungle survival training. Didn't do too well, did I?"

"You protected your poor feet," the priest said. "You found your way out of the jungle."

"How do I find my way out of all this?"

"We will try."

21
PRIEST IN DISGUISE

Jimmie awoke on Tuesday morning around six. Too early to call the Garcías? Although probably no one in that house would have slept.

Victoria had made coffee. While drinking it, they listened to news by radio and heard that Graciela García was missing: a pretty girl of nineteen, five feet four, wearing a white skirt and blouse and straw sandals, carrying a straw handbag embroidered in blue and orange. A car registered in her name had been found late last night at the plaza near the *Presidencia*.

What an untelling reduction of Graci's self, Jimmie thought, to the time measure of a news item – and how false the continuation was: "Police think it is too soon for alarm. Many girls drop out of sight, for romantic reasons, for a night or so."

She remembered something forgotten: last night, after Muñoz had gone, Graci had said, "I tried to call you when I got your message."

But there had been no message; Jimmie had not called Graciela. Last night she had been too much shocked by Muñoz to speculate about what that call might have meant. And by the time Graci had come to the apartment, the damage had been done: whoever had telephoned would have known where Graciela was, would have had to wait only until she went out to her car to go home.

The almond pastry that Vicky had put on the table had been a favorite of John Chilton's. Jimmie could not eat it.

The ivory-colored Frangi watched them from a third chair at the table.

"He cried, Miss Jimmie. He jumped up on my bed and tears were running out of his eyes. He knows things are wrong."

Jimmie telephoned at seven and was answered at once by the lawyer.

"Another call," he said. "If I deliver your uncle's papers by Saturday noon, Graciela will be returned."

"What else can you do? My uncle would not have let anything happen to Graci."

"We have four days," García said grimly. "The papers are not my possession. San Martín and I are working together. Though he has his own trouble – you heard that Ahora has been shut down?"

"Oh no!"

"Yesterday."

"What else can happen?"

"What can happen is that San Martín and I will fight."

"Your wife – is she – not all right – but –"

"Keeping her bravery," García said. "Keep yours, señorita. One of my associates, the young Tomás, will help you if you need him. Tomorrow, I will not be able to come to read the will, but Tomás will be there." He gave Jimmie the name of the Episcopal minister who would deliver short prayers at the funeral home and at the burial, in case Father Luis could not come.

"Prayers – yes. And we will be thinking prayers for Graciela."

"Señorita, if you would please eat something –" Vicky said.

"Vicky, I will sometime. I must call Father Luis. The burial will be tomorrow. And señor García has four days –"

The doorbell rang. Victoria opened the door for Roberto.

"Jimmie." How tall and thin she was in

the dark blue long dressing gown. But she looked at him with hope, warmth.

"I have just heard about Graciela. I am – well, desolated."

Jimmie told him of the message García had received.

"The Condor. Damn them. And it's the Condor that has shut down Ahora. I don't know if you've heard. I talked with San Martín – padlocked into the street this morning when he went to his offices. And his printer won't work for him. But we won't give in – never. We're a civilized country – these things are appalling – more so, more visible in a small country – but there are people, forces here that *must* put them down!" He struck the edge of the table with his fist, then, controlling himself, said to Jimmie: "What can I do for you?"

She told him of the arrangements for tomorrow.

"Is your sister coming today?"

"I don't know. She and Glenn are feuding with me. They demand that Uncle John should be buried in the Zone. Ghastly, Roberto. Haggling – Glenn doesn't approve –"

"Doesn't approve of murder in Panama?" Roberto said.

If I never do anything else, Roberto

152

thought, I have made them laugh. For Jimmie and Vicky laughed, even if thinly.

"On target," Jimmie said. "Now if we can get through tomorrow – without a fight beside the coffin –" she shivered.

"García won't be with you – do you want me?"

I will always want you, Jimmie thought. Forever and ever.

"García is sending an associate who will help me today if I need him. I must call Father Luis. Must order flowers – Uncle John didn't want a funeral – but he liked flowers. He couldn't mind that, could he?"

"No. And I will call Father Luis."

She gave Roberto the priest's telephone number, the address of the funeral home, and the time of the service – of what service there would be. "But Roberto, please tell him – if he can't easily come – Uncle John would have understood. I understand. And if he can come – we will want him to stay here, or if there is some problem – decorum or such craziness – maybe you'd help?"

"Of course. I'll make it proper. He can stay with me."

She told Roberto, then, of Colonel Muñoz's visit to the apartment the night before.

"If only I had gone in with you! Vicky –

don't leave her alone, will you?"

"No. Not even to bring her food."

"Call me if you need food," Roberto said.

She followed Roberto to the door. "I keep thinking – what Uncle John would have said about – all this. Vultures fighting for shreds –"

"Stop it," Roberto said. He hugged her as he left.

In the yellow house Roberto, to his surprise, found all three servants. The cook had prepared his breakfast, which Ahmad served. Eduardo, he said, had gone out very early. To Paula on her way to the laundry with a basket of clothes, Roberto said, "We may have a guest tonight or tomorrow. Please clean the blue guest room. And see that there is food that can be served quickly. Cold meats – wine – fruit."

Paula looked interest. "A lady?"

"A priest."

"Que lástima."

"I know you would like to cook up something romantic, Paula. But this will be a special priest. Flowers, brandy, biscuits in his room. Make sure the bedside lamp works. Best towels in his bathroom – if we have any."

"All fairly worn. Ragged. But I will do what I can."

"Where is my aunt?"

"Sleeping, señor. Oh, and Señor San Martín telephoned. He will call again."

Around ten San Martín telephoned again.

"Roberto, I am sending by messenger the copy for the sheet – shall we call it Ahorita? Make any changes you want to. Later – after the Xerox – I will help in distributing. But Roberto, they have crippled me. No files, no morgue. Padlocks. Guards. If only I could remember –"

"What, Carlos?"

"A place – vacation place – that Muñoz used to have. Years back. Maybe he still has it. It's a long shot, but I have a feeling about Muñoz. Meanwhile, García and I are working on another idea. He cannot leave his house because another call may come from the kidnaper. Nor does he want to leave his wife. But I am scouring the streets to find my newsboys. They are everywhere. Shining shoes, begging, running errands. I use – have used – about twenty of them. Mostly from the Chorillo district. But you find them throughout the city. Elusive, sometimes almost invisible, skilled in evading the *Guardia*. Some of them pickpockets. Well. I find them honest and dependable. They found out last night that Ahora would not

155

publish. Which will send them lurking, scurrying, trying to make a few *centavos* in any way they can. Poor little devils."

"And you think," Roberto said, "that one of your boys might have seen something last night, or heard something about the kidnaping?"

"Yes. The homeless ones sleep in the plazas. Graci's car was found at the plaza near your house. I believe there is a chance. I have sent out the word – I want as many of the boys as possible to come to my house. Several have arrived already. I am offering a reward for any information they can give. And food for all of them. I have included a note about the reward in the sheet I'm sending you."

"Excellent," Roberto said. "Out of thirty boys, one or more might help us. But now find out about Muñoz's retreat? Do we need a break into your offices to use your files?"

"I'm considering that," San Martín said grimly.

"I would help."

Over a faulty telephone connection, Roberto heard Father Luis's words faintly but recognized distress in the priest's tones.

"Yes, Roberto. I remember meeting you. How is the señorita?"

Roberto gave him Jimmie's messages.

"But of course I will come. Even if it must be sub rosa – and not in my usual clothing. Even if I have to borrow something to wear – and hitchhike – my rather ancient car will not run. And my bicycle is not much healthier. I sometimes think of buying a mule."

"I will come for you, *Padre*. I will try to leave by three. And I will want you to stay with me tonight, tomorrow night, too."

"You are kind, Roberto. But there is –"

The rest of the sentence was obscured.

"I can't hear you, *Padre.*"

"There is someone here who is ill – I do not think I can be away for a night."

"I will bring a boy who works for us. He will stay with your patient. And I will bring you something to wear."

"There is a problem here – about my patient. I shall need to see señor García."

"You have heard that señor García's daughter has been kidnaped?"

"*Madre de dios* – no!"

"But you will be able to see señor García's associate."

There was a silence.

"Are you there, *Padre?*"

"Yes. Yes, Roberto. I will come today."

Ahmad, wakened from a nap in the shade under the house, made no objection to
157

accompanying Roberto to Natá; although a Moslem, he sympathized with an infidel's need for a holy man, and he welcomed his release from regular duties for a day or two. He gave Roberto an endearing smile and went back to sleep.

"Que muchacho!" Paula exclaimed, half-critical, half-affectionate. She was gathering purple and white flowers for the priest's room. Roberto persuaded the cook to be on duty that evening and the next day.

San Martín's carefully typed legal-sized sheet arrived shortly afterward: it contained, in the center, a terse announcement of the discontinuance of Ahora. At the sides were columns, one offering a reward for information about the kidnapping, another concerning Chilton's murder. At the foot of the sheet a brief signed editorial note urged restraint from any demonstrations in reaction to the Canal Treaties.

Roberto made 300 copies on the Xerox machine in García's offices; took some to be distributed by fellow-students at the University; paid other students to leave copies in buses, on park benches, in restaurants; sent Ahmad to give out copies at the market. He himself left copies in coffee shops, restaurants, and three hotels.

It was four o'clock before he had time to

take a copy of the Xeroxed sheet to Jimmie. He found Victoria waiting for his arrival before going to the market.

"If you take your list to Paula, she'll do your marketing in the morning. Anything you need tonight?"

"No. Just for tomorrow – when people will be here. Thank you, señor. I will go over now."

To Jimmie he said. "Go out on the terrace. I will bring you a drink. You look rather beat up. And no wonder. Hard day."

"García's Tomás helped me all through. You look kind of beat yourself. Tell you what – you make me a drink and I'll make you one. And no – don't hug me or I'll cry on your shoulder."

"You'd better not. This is my last clean white shirt. How do you stay so cool looking?"

"Because I'm afraid. Of the *Guardia*, damn them. And afraid for Graci."

"So am I," Roberto said soberly. A breeze from the marina and the shade of thick vines growing from the base of the railing to the roof cooled the accumulated heat of late afternoon.

"I can stay only a few minutes," Roberto said. "I'm driving to Natá to bring back Father Luis. He has no way of coming,

159

though he was determined to get there somehow. He sounded troubled – has somebody with him who's ill. I'm taking Ahmad with me to stay all night with the patient. The poor old *padre* – can't wear his clerical garb into town. His superiors don't want him here. Wonder how he will look in my clothes. Paula's trying to catch up with the laundry, but right now about all I can produce would be yellow slacks and an orange checked shirt. Think he could give a prayer in an outfit like that?"

"Yes. He could. But you're so much taller – how about something of Uncle John's?" She called Vicky, who had returned from the yellow house. "Uncle John had a white suit, didn't he? It's laundered?"

"Yes, Miss Jimmie."

"Would you pack it – and white shoes – and a hat? And dark glasses? They're for Father Luis."

"That nice old man," Vicky said. "I remember the last time he was here. He was so worried. Some priest over him had tried to make him do something he wouldn't do."

"Do you remember the other priest's name?" Roberto asked.

"Father Sebastian. I wasn't really listening – cleaning up – but I heard some things they were saying, your uncle and the *padre*. And

I do remember how your uncle looked after the *padre* left. Sat there, thinking and looking in the way he did when he had got an idea. Miss Jimmie – your uncle never never got cross, even if you interrupted him while he was thinking."

"Oh damn damn," Jimmie said, and ground at her eyes with a handkerchief. She controlled her grief and said to Roberto, "Do you know this Father Sebastian?"

"I've seen him. Met him somewhere – with Eduardo. Looks like Richelieu but meaner. Big wheel in the Church. Well, one thing: they can't defrock *Padre* Luis for coming to make his prayer – he already defrocked. Good idea, the dark glasses."

"Now you," he said to Jimmie when Victoria brought him a small traveling bag, "you take it easy. Keep all doors locked. If I'm not too late getting back, I'll call you."

"Call me – even if you're too late."

But it was too late when Roberto brought Father Luis to the yellow house. Only a small night light showed in the apartment.

On the drive to Panama City they had talked. Enough for Roberto to share the priest's perplexity about the injured soldier.

"It was like an involuntary confession, Roberto. I don't know what I should do. Certainly the boy has evidence about the crime. He has that belt – he saw the figure propped up in the chair beside the window. He took some of the coins. He is being searched for by the United States Army, by the *Guardia*. How fair would they be? Do I have the right to make public his story?"

And the trip along the coast on board the *Isla* – the cases he had seen unloaded, Roberto thought unhappily.

"If you could get the boy to turn himself in to a lawyer," he said to the priest. If not García, someone else in his firm?

"I tried to persuade him to do that. But so much of the time he has been delirious."

An unhappy trip. *Padre* Luis had looked like a shrunken parody of John Chilton. A revenant. But the priest had a vital spirit, even if trammeled by what Roberto thought were long years of subservience to dogmatic superiors. How then explain the books he had seen in the cottage at Natá – books by Kierkegaard, Proust, Voltaire, Marx, a biography of Cárdenas?

They had been silent for many miles before Father Luis said, "I hope your Ahmad will remember to feed Negrito."

"He will. Ahmad likes cats."

"It was kind, Roberto, to bring food – the sandwiches, the fruit, the cake, the thermos jugs with milk and coffee."

162

The yellow house had been empty when they arrived.

The knocking at his door woke Roberto hours later. Before he could respond, Eduardo and his aunt had come into his room.

"Roberto," Teresa cried, "who is in the blue guestroom? I opened the door – for more air – and saw someone on the bed – *who?*"

"A friend of mine."

"What friend?" Eduardo demanded. "A woman?"

"No," Roberto said. "If it were – would I be sleeping alone?"

"If you do not tell us, we will wake this person and find out who he is," Teresa threatened.

"I live here too," Roberto said. "If I want to have a guest – what of it?"

"Very well, Eduardo, go wake that person."

"Wait. Wait, both of you. My guest is a priest."

Eduardo, with a flashlight, had already gone to the guestroom. He came back, saying, "You are lying, Roberto. The clothing is not that of a priest."

Behind Eduardo a quiet voice said, "My friends, please do not be disturbed."

Father Luis, in a gray bathrobe of Roberto's which restored to him something clerical, even monkish, faced Teresa in her yellow evening gown and Eduardo in a sky-blue dinner jacket, and spoke with gentle authority.

"I am a priest. I am Father Luis but I am here in a private cause. I have accepted hospitality from my friend Roberto for this night but shall leave tomorrow."

If he had drawn a circle and pronounced the curse of excommunication, he could hardly have silenced the others more forcefully.

"Forgive us, *Padre,*" Teresa said. Eduardo, bowed.

Roberto, sitting up in bed, in faded grey-striped pajamas, felt outside the pageantry.

"Now," Father Luis said, "this boy –" he gestured toward Roberto – "needs to rest. I ask you to leave us."

When they had gone, Roberto got out of bed and lighted a cigarette. "Sorry, *Padre.*"

The priest laughed. "Did I overdo the act?"

"No. But it was impressive. Can you sleep now?"

"I think not. But you?"

"No." Roberto was already on his way downstairs. "I will make coffee."

164

After coffee and rolls, they dressed and at Father Luis's suggestion went out into the five o'clock coolness. The lights in the pale domed *Presidencia* were dim; they saw no guards. A night light in Jimmie's apartment still burned. In the fragrant pre-dawn they came to sit on a stone bench in the plaza beyond the yellow house.

"Your family," the priest said, "is attractive. I believe I have met your brother – I think he is a friend of Monsignor Sebastian, my superior. The lady?"

"My aunt Teresa. They have many invitations. To some they go together. As tonight, I imagine." He thought, Eduardo looks older than my aunt. And more tired than ever, after a party. Then thinking of something else, he laughed. "You have an advantage, *Padre:* with a tonsure you can get up looking very neat."

"A perquisite of the priesthood," the *padre* said.

Trucks delivering milk, bread and rolls, newspapers, began to run; around six the sun with its immoderate equatorial speed emerged over the marina and began to braise the white yachts, the houses facing the water.

"One thing," Roberto said. "I want to tell

San Martín – you know of him – the publisher of Ahora?"

"Yes."

"You know that Ahora has been shut down. But we are circulating a Xeroxed sheet. I want to tell him that someone – a possible witness – holds evidence concerning señor Chilton's murder. No name. Perhaps we can say that the informant will deliver himself into his lawyer's charge. We might get some action. From the enemy."

"Let us hope the enemy does not find this possible witness," Father Luis said. "Well, if you can take me back to Natá this afternoon –"

"Yes. I will try to start by mid-afternoon."

He saw, stopping at the yellow house, a car from which Paula and the cook got out.

"Will you come back with me for breakfast, *Padre?* Or would you rather go to the Chilton apartment?"

"To the apartment, I think. If it is not too early."

"No. And *Padre,* would you please tell Jimmie that I will call her or see her – tonight, if I can?"

22
UNREST IN THE CANAL ZONE

"I will not," Tom Furniss said, "go to that funeral."

Clay Austin was driving him to school. Glenn had had to go early to his office; Isabel needed the second car to go to her sister.

"Well," Clay said, "who's making you?"

"Are you going?"

"Too much to do here. By the way, how did you get that black eye?"

"Had a fight with a kid at school," Tom said. "The crazy bastard said Panama should get the Canal."

From a hilltop they saw, evenly spaced, three ships crawling along the invisible water of the Canal as if they were truncated land vehicles moving between two walls of jungle toward the Caribbean.

"That's what we are supposed to give up," Tom said. "I'd rather blow up the whole Canal than see it handed over to Panama."

"You'd blow it up?" Clay smiled. "You and who else?"

167

"Never mind. Those kids back in '64 – they got in some wallops. Started the riots, didn't they? I was a baby. But my father told me about it. And those kids hadn't had any fight training. It'll be a damned disgrace if we get kicked out of the Zone."

"We're not kicked out yet," Clay said as he left Tom at school. "I'll pick you up this afternoon."

When he went into the Administration building, he found that the unrestful activity of the past weeks had intensified.

"The Governor *would* make up his mind this morning to fly to Washington," Glenn said at the doorway to Clay's office. "Everybody's trying to see him – they get pushed off on me. And of all days – I've got to go to Chilton's funeral or Isabel will – God knows what she'd do. Can't blame her. I was going to ask you to go with us."

"Impossible," Clay said. "I'll do what I can here."

"I'll get back as soon as I can this afternoon. You'll have to tell people the Governor isn't making any more appointments." He looked at his watch. "He's pulling out in an hour. There goes my telephone again. Take it, Clay – it's probably some captain at the base – keeps calling – wants us to pressure the Panamanians to step up the hunt for that

168

deserter. As if we'd get any cooperation right now. I've got to leave."

Clay took the call and told the captain that all possible pressure would be exerted on the government of Panama.

Around three-thirty Glenn returned to deal with a dozen or more perplexed and irritated civil servants. Shortly after his return, Clay left to pick up Tom and drive him home.

23
SANCTUARY

"Before you finish today's new sheet," Roberto said, telephoning to San Martín, "I want to see you. All right if I come now – or are you too busy with newsboys – and any luck with them?"

"Maybe. I've narrowed the horde down to four who were near the plaza Monday night. One of them I think knows something. He's scared – hasn't talked yet. Come along whenever you want to."

They talked in San Martín's study.

"My wife is doing a good job winning them over. Better job than I did last night

169

breaking into my own offices. Oh, I got in all right – a window at the rear has a loose lock. But the Condor has been there ahead of me. All files, the morgue cleaned out. I think they even took what was in the waste baskets. Well. We're getting dozens of calls. From readers of yesterday's sheet. Encouraging support. For as long as the Condor doesn't do something else. Probably not today, with all the fuss about the old politician's funeral. What's new with you?"

Roberto told him what he had learned from Father Luis and of his conversation with the priest in the early morning. Together he and San Martín finished the preparation of the news sheet. Before leaving, Roberto asked whether any word had come from García.

"He called this morning. Another call – the same voice – reminding him that Saturday was coming, saying he would receive instructions about the papers. Also warning that García was not to take any action through the police or any other agency. Graciela, the man said, was being cared for. García asked for proof that she was alive. But the caller hung up. García is checking real estate transactions, tax records – we both think Muñoz is involved. He knew Graciela had been with señorita Jimmie –

170

knew where to find her. Probably he or one of his men had made that call to Graci. If we can get some lead to places Muñoz owns – man like that is bound to have hideaways to entertain ladies or non-ladies."

"Or," Roberto said grimly, "if we could get a lead to a lady or non-lady."

"No hope there. I imagine they'd be pretty well paid. Or have other reasons for silence."

The pomp of the old politician's funeral, held a short time after the brief prayers and burial of John Chilton, brought heavy traffic. Roberto was impeded, halted more than once, in making contact with the friends who would help to distribute the copies of the news sheet, so that he was later than he had expected to be when he picked up Father Luis, who was waiting for him inside the door of the apartment building.

"Jimmie," the priest said as they drove out of the city, "was behaving with soldierly fortitude."

"Or priestly? I know she was grateful to you."

"The poor child is apparently having difficulties with her sister and her brother-in-law, who seemed to disapprove throughout the reading of the will. I did not think I should be present, but she seemed to want

171

me there. And I had to stay. There was a particularly moving embarrasing moment for me, well, really two. One was when the young lawyer read of a fine and generous legacy to me. And the second was when a great truck deposited two enormous containers, addressed to señor Chilton, at the outer door. The reading was interrupted. I went down with the señorita and recognized from the labels that these boxes contained forty pairs of roller skates."

"Roller skates!" Roberto exclaimed.

"Yes. For the boys in a club I started while I was still here."

"Were some of the boys newsboys?"

"Many of them."

"I must tell San Martín," Roberto said, and explained: the roller skates might help persuade the newsboys to give any information they had concerning Graciela's kidnaping.

He gave the priest a copy of this day's news sheet.

"I hope we are doing the right thing, Roberto. I hope that the young soldier will not feel that we have betrayed him by mentioning a possible witness. And by that notice asking for information if anyone finds the snakeskin belt."

"We haven't told where he is. And only

the murderer would know about the belt."

Meanwhile, Jimmie, alone with Victoria after the departure of Isabel and Glenn and the lawyer Tomás but not yet ready to rest, worried about the disposition of the great cases of roller skates, which the truck driver said were too large to be conveyed to the basement of the building.

"Señor Roberto will think of something," Victoria said. "The boy Ahmad might unpack them and make trips with a car to take them to Chorillo. The old building where the boys had their club – he could take them there. The boxes can stay at the door overnight – they are too big to be stolen."

At five-thirty the telephone rang in Jimmie's apartment. Jimmie answered. A cold authoritative voice asked for Father Luis.

"He is not here. Who is calling, please?"

"I am Father Sebastian. I understand that he was in the city today. If he is not there – where is he?"

"I do not know."

A pause. Then the voice said, "Señorita, of course you are lying. Is he in Natá or on his way there?"

"I don't know where he is," Jimmie said.

"Very well. We will assume that he is in Natá. We will also assume that you

173

are involved in a priest's flaunting of authority."

"I think," Jimmie said to Victoria, "I'm about to be excommunicated from a Church I don't belong to. But Father Luis – oh, great. If that old weirdo sends his people out to bring back the priest – they'll find the soldier."

She called the priest's number and was answered by Ahmad.

"Have the *padre* and señor Roberto come?"

"No, señorita."

"Ahmad, I think the priest's superior is sending people to bring him back to the city. They mustn't find the soldier. Will you hide him?"

"Yes, but where?"

"Is the church near?"

"Near, yes, but within sight of people. The old woman who cooks for the *padre* is curious."

"Before anyone can get there," Jimmie said, "it will be dark. As soon as it is dark, take the soldier into the church. Hide him – in the vestiary – under robes – you know where the vestiary is? The room where priests put on their robes?"

"I'll find it. I would be more familiar with a mosque, señorita."

174

"And Ahmad – make the soldier give you that snakeskin belt – and hide it. In case they find him. They must not find the belt."

"Separating him from the belt will be like tearing the lashes from a fish's eye," Ahmad said. "But I will do it."

Still almost a half-hour before darkness, Ahmad saw from the position of the sun. Cliff was sleeping. No one moved in Natá. He fed the cat, of whom he had grown fond, brought water from the well, watched the approach to the cottage by road, and wandered across the flower-flanked square to the church. The main door was unlocked; inside, beyond the alter, a door which he supposed shut off the vestiary, was locked; but, returning to the cottage, he found the priest's keys, unlocked the vestiary.

Around six, when darkness was about to close down, he woke Cliff.

"Up, boy. You're going into the church. Here is a soutane. Put it on."

"Why, for god's sake?"

"Because people are coming – you've got to hide – and because there's a street light between here and the church."

"What people are coming?"

"Anybody coming – anybody who finds you – no good. Come on. Into the black robe. Off with the snakeskin belt."

"Off like hell. This belt could save my life."

"Yes, idiot, if you had it. But we don't know what the people who are coming will do."

Ahmad helped Cliff out of bed, robed him in the black soutane, and when the sun had set, helped him to walk to the church. Anyone watching would have seen a lame priest supported by a slim foreign-looking young man, limping toward the church. The interior smelled fragrant from ancient wood, incense, and flowers.

"Now." Ahmad said, opening the door to the vestiary. "You lie down behind that chest. And give me that belt."

"I won't," Cliff said. "I've never been in a Catholic church. Not all my life."

"I haven't either," Ahmad said. "Does that mean we can't use one when we need it? You trust me?"

"Yes," Cliff said. He gave Ahmad a smile that broke through all Ahmad's reserve biases against infidels, although he had liked many and trusted some.

He touched Cliff's forehead: hot. The fever was returning. He pulled a robe from the chest, spread it out, forced Cliff to lie down. He placed a white and gold cloth over the top of the chest so that it hung down and

176

covered Cliff. Then he brought a jar of water from the well and set it on the floor at the end of the chest.

"Go to sleep, boy. There's water here if you need it."

Cliff was already asleep. In the darkness Ahmad fumbled for the belt buckle, removed the belt, and hid it in a long-handled box he had found earlier. He replaced the box with others in a rack, and went back through the church, wondering why the churches of infidels had so many secretive places, so much equipment – those bottles, jars, odd little glasses in round trays, the chest of robes and cloth coverings. A devious sect, he thought. A mosque seemed clean and bare in contrast to a church.

At the door of the priest's cottage Negrito yowled quietly in greeting.

"Are you a Christian, cat?" Ahmad said.

Negrito looked at him through yellow slanted eyes, noncommittally.

An hour or so later, Roberto and the priest found Ahmad asleep on the bed and no sign of Cliff.

"Ahmad," Roberto said. "Where is the soldier?"

Ahmad sat up. "Safe. Hidden in the church. But you are late, señor. I tried to stay awake."

"We didn't come here directly," Roberto said. He did not explain the deviation from their route to Natá. While the daylight lasted, he and Father Luis had gone to Coclé, where the priest, wirily muscular, had helped him to scale the wall. With tools that he had brought, Roberto had first forced open a low doorway in the canvas-topped building, and with a flashlight had entered a clay-floored windowless room, which was underground for three-fourths of its height, a dank cold room furnished with a table, three chairs, and a small locked filing cabinet. A half-full bottle of brandy and three small glasses stood on the table.

Next he had forced the padlock on the shed. He would not soon forget the dismay in the priest's face at what they had seen, or the immediacy of his own recognition of what he himself must do.

Father Luis had groped for the rosary concealed under the secular shirt.

"Roberto! We must report this to a government authority?"

Roberto shook his head. "No, Father. The people who call themselves the Condor – they must be responsible for this. But we don't know how many others are involved. If the head of state were here, it would be different. But he is out of the country. We don't know who could be trusted."

"But Roberto, what can we do?"

"You will pray."

"Yes, for the city. The country. But Roberto, is there time to wait for an answer to prayers?"

Roberto had not answered, for he did not know how soon the most devout expected prayers to be answered by a deity probably overtaxed by supplications. But he would have been less than honest if he had denied an unreasoning comfort from the priest's presence and intentions.

Now in the cottage at Natá he faced the problem of Father Luis's safety. Ahmad had told of Jimmie's call.

"Padre," Roberto said. "If they come – what will happen to you?"

"Nothing that will interfere with what I believe," the priest said. "But I am surprised. I did not think anyone recognized me."

"We could – maybe a wild idea – but we *could* make a dash for the Costa Rican border – get you out of the country."

"But not out of my allegiance to my Church and to my superiors – however much I disagree with them. No. The danger is for the soldier. If I am taken back to the city, what will happen to him?"

"I'll take care of him. Somehow," Roberto said.

Ahmad was making tea, preparing sandwiches which he brought to the others.

"Roberto," the priest said, "you could go back – avoid involvement."

"No. I'm staying. Until we know whether you are to be taken to the city. Until I can think what to do about Cliff. Of course, Jimmie might have been wrong. Maybe no one will come tonight."

The priest shook his head."

"They will not delay," he said. "I know how they operate." He went into the bedroom and exchanged the suit he wore for his usual garb. "If I have to go, I will go as a priest."

And as a priest he went, a little later, when two emissaries from Father Sebastian came to the cottage. At the first sound of an approaching car, Roberto sent Ahmad to the church. But the emissaries had no interest in anyone except the priest.

When they had gone, Roberto went to the church, where he found Ahmad squatting inside the main doorway. In the vestiary Cliff slept under the gold and white altar cloth.

"Come along now, Cliff." He roused the boy, helped him to walk toward the front of the church.

"The belt!" Cliff cried. "Where is it?"

"Ahmad will bring it. We're going to the city."

The cat, Roberto thought – what about him? But Ahmad was already putting the cat into the car, beside a paper bag holding the snakeskin belt.

On the back seat, Cliff went to sleep as Roberto started the car toward Panama City.

"Where are you going to take him?" Ahmad asked.

"I haven't decided."

"I have a small room. In my brother Ali's house, over his bakery. I could keep Cliff there. And the cat."

"But what happens to you – if he is found there?"

"He won't be found. The house connects with another – he will be safe. Police never come. They can't understand our language – and if they do come, we speak only Indonesian."

24
CHILTON'S NOTES

On the morning after the day of the funeral, Jimmie and Victoria began the unhappy work of packing Chilton's clothing. Victoria was to take whatever her relatives could use, and the rest would be sent with the roller skates to the boys' club that Father Luis had started in the Chorillo district.

The desk in the study looked bleak without the humanizing bits of notes, the pens, the opened letters that it had borne while Chilton lived. Letters that had come since Sunday were banded, waiting until Jimmie had time to answer them; the note pads put into a drawer – note pad – Jimmie remembered, now, as she polished the desk, that she had put a pad with her uncle's last notes, into the pocket of a sweater she had worn that dreadful Sunday night – Monday morning.

"Yes," Vicky said. "I have that blue sweater – to be laundered." She brought the pad from the sweater pocket; and Jimmie, after reading the notes, went to the telephone.

Paula answered.

"Oh, Miss Jimmie," Paula said, half sobbing. "Have you seen the paper this morning? It's Laura."

"I haven't looked at the paper," Jimmie said.

"She was my friend – she worked for a Mr. Austin in the Canal Zone. Last night – her husband was coming to meet her at the wire fence – at the boundary – he found her beaten. Terribly. He says someone ran away. She is in a hospital. They don't know whether she will live."

"Horrible," Jimmie said. "Laura. Yes, I remember her. She helped my sister's maid. That Sunday. That pretty girl!"

Paula wept.

"Vicky," Jimmie said, coming away from the telephone. "Maybe you should go to the yellow house – Paula is really shook – you saw the paper?"

"About Laura? Yes," Vicky said. "I didn't want to trouble you – so early."

"If Roberto comes please ask him to call me."

It had been too late to call when Roberto, after leaving Cliff and the cat with Ahmad, returned to the yellow house; and too early to call this morning when he had tooled open one of the cartons of roller skates and taken six pairs to San Martín. The editor seemed more cheerful than Roberto felt.

"The skates might just turn the trick, Roberto. We've got a home here for stray newsboys – lucky my wife likes and understands children. And I have the news copy ready."

"Have you heard from García?"

"Yes. He's getting some action from Captain Reyes and has hired a private detective. His wife has pretty much collapsed. He took her to the hospital last night."

"This is the critical day," Roberto said. "The Condor may try to balk our distribution. Watch yourself, Carlos. They have Father Luis. Took him last night after he got back to Natá."

"What are they trying to do – revive the Inquisition?"

"God knows," Roberto said wearily. "At least the soldier is safe. For the moment."

"It would be a good time for the Condor to make a strike. And something is under way. Unfortunate city rabble are stirred up. Our head of government left the country on some mission last night. And one of my reporters – still working – tells me the

Governor of the Zone flew to Washington yesterday. School kids in the Zone are beginning to drive around with American flags. Like 1964. Which you don't remember. But they started the riots. If that poor girl that got more than half-killed at the boundary last night weren't just another West Indian, an incident might have sprouted out of that. You heard about it on the radio?"

"Yes. But an incident – you mean against the Zone? But it was at the boundary. And I don't see how the Condor could be involved."

"You can't tell," San Martín said.

How, Roberto wondered, can you be so cheerful? But you are a fighter. I am not a fighter. And whatever I try to do seems to lead me into an abyss of doubt and fear about Eduardo. He knew I was sheltering a priest here on Tuesday night. Oh Eduardo, he thought, I do not want it to have been you who caused the priest's apprehension. But whoever was responsible, the fact remained that Father Luis would be under something like house arrest; the soldier's situation uncertain; Graciela in captivity; the head of the government away, and the whole country threatened with upheaval.

God damn it, they won't get away with it.

185

I'm not a fighter, but I'll plod through this.

I would also, he thought, feel better if I had some breakfast. There had been no time last night for dinner.

He had taken three steps away from the outer door of San Martín's apartment house when two aggressively starched members of the *Guardia* got out of a car and approached him.

"Señor, we will take that envelope," the senior of the two said.

"On what authority?" Roberto asked. But he knew it was a losing battle. The policeman produced a paper – Roberto saw a scrawled signature of a magistrate – saw also, under the casually open blouses of their uniforms, the holstered revolvers, the hands touching the butts. He surrendered the envelope.

"So," he said bitterly, "the Condor has sent out orders."

The younger policeman, falsely puzzled, said, "The Condor – who is that?"

His older companion said, "Where is your faith in the unseen, my boy?" To Roberto he said, "Naturally we all know there is a Condor. Depending on your views –" he shrugged – "it could be good or bad for the country. At any rate, we take our orders from superiors who themselves take orders from men higher up, perhaps men in contact with

186

the Condor? But no matter how far down in the scale, many of us knew and loved the old politician who was buried yesterday. If he was the Condor – or one of the Condors – then many of us would follow the orders of the Condor."

"Even if those orders contradicted the policies of the head of state – Torrijos?" Roberto asked.

"We have not had to face that question, señor."

"Then get ready to," Roberto said curtly.

The yellow house, when he returned dispiritedly, was silent. Teresa was probably upstairs asleep. Eduardo's car was not in the parking space. At least, Roberto thought, I'll have time to see Jimmie.

The *abrazo* with which he greeted Jimmie at the apartment door was not casual.

"Roberto – I have been longing to see you!" She added quickly, "I have found some notes of Uncle John's – they may tell us something."

"You haven't had breakfast, Mr. Roberto," Victoria said. "Paula has gone to the hospital – her friend Laura was hurt last night."

"I know," Roberto said gloomily. "And no, I haven't had breakfast or any other food for ages."

"You're going to have one of Vicky's super omelets," Jimmie said. "Sit down – I'll show you the notes."

Victoria brought the omelet, with bacon, hot rolls, iced papaya slices, and coffee, while Roberto was studying the fragmentary note on the little pad: Resee C.G. on any sh. mvments. to harb. Coc. coast."

"C.G. – Coast Guard," Roberto translated. "Ship movements to harbor – Coclé coast. Yes. I will do that."

"At the foot of the top page," Jimmie said, "he started another note." She read it.

As Izaak Walton might have said, whilst
fishes rarely escape, the angler may,
as the man of the River.

"Then blank," Jimmie said. "Was he interrupted?"

"Fish? Fishes?" Roberto frowned.

"Vicky," Jimmie said. "When Uncle John made little notes like these – do you know what he did with them?"

"I think," Vicky said, "he crossed them out. In red. When he had done something about them. He used to tear them up. I remember the red lines when I threw them away with the trash."

"Here's something, farther back in

188

the pad," Roberto said. "Not in his abbreviations." He read:

> Whose the hand will plunge the knife
> That brings cessation to my life?
> Priest, fighter, ancient knave
> Or ghost – who'll send me to my grave?

Jimmie tore at her hair. "He foresaw something – foresaw –"

"Steady, *querida*," Roberto said.

Victoria, refilling his coffee cup, shook her head sadly. "More of those things he used to write. One time, I was dusting the study, and he said, 'Vicky, if you think I've gone senile and am writing poetry, you're wrong. Sometimes I take notes in jingles – helps to view a situation.' I didn't understand what he meant, but I liked to hear him."

"I understand some of this," Roberto said. "Father Sebastian, Muñoz, the old man buried yesterday – they were the Condor. The ghost – someone out of his past?"

"Or if the third member of the Condor died," Jimmie said, "would there be a new member? The ghost?"

Roberto frowned.

"Roberto, can't we work together? To find who murdered him?"

"Yes. But only, Jimmie, if you will

promise to stay within safe limits."

"To hell with safe limits! He was my uncle! Where do we begin?"

"With the Coast Guard. I know an officer. I'll see him today."

Fish, he thought again. There was the ritual burial of a fish in Panama City on the last night of the pre-Lenten Carnival. No. He saw no connection there. Maybe I should try writing verses, he thought, for a new angle of analysis.

Roberto took time to tell Jimmie what had happened, as far as he knew, to Father Luis and to the soldier; also what San Martín and García were doing. He explained why he had broken out some of the skates, promised to have the others taken away.

"And your paper?" Jimmie asked.

"The copy was confiscated this morning by the *Guardia*," Roberto said bitterly. "I must call San Martín. He'll know somebody in the Coast Guard to check with. May I use your phone?"

Why, he wondered, after he made the call, had he not wanted to telephone from the yellow house? He had not tried to keep secret his work on San Martín's sheets. His aunt, Eduardo, must know about it. I don't know, he thought. Only – oh, *dios*, I have loved that house. But it no longer seems friendly. Stop it, he thought. It's my home. I've never lived anywhere else.

"So, what's the best thing for me to do?" Jimmie asked.

"We have to find out what is happening to Father Luis. I don't know what we could do – but we must know. Could you dress very Spanish – and try to see him? Pretend you're a cousin? It's a huge complex – monastery, convent, school, cathedral. I can't go – too many people there know me – I've met the priests through my father and Eduardo. There will be a lot of visitors there today – from all over Latin America – because of the funeral of the old rogue yesterday. He had his connections."

"Of course I'll go," Jimmie said. "I'll get black clothes from Felix Maduro's store – shall I be a cousin from Spain?"

"I think that would be best."

"And then what, Roberto?"

"There's Cliff. The soldier. As far as we know, he's safe with Ahmad and his Indonesians. But we have to get Cliff into a lawyer's custody – keep him free to give testimony. But that's for me to do."

"Would it be safer if Cliff stayed here?" Jimmie asked.

"I don't think so. The *Guardia* might decide to make another search. Cliff's

191

description has been circulated in the papers."

"All right," Jimmie said. "I'll try to see the padre – then what?"

"I must see García. His house is probably being watched – we'll have to do some more disguising to smuggle Cliff into it. If only I knew somebody in the U.S. Army – somebody I could trust to protect Cliff –"

"I know the Governor of the Zone," Jimmie said.

"Who is now out of the country."

"I don't suppose Glenn could help. Even if Isabel put on the heat – poor-homesick-boy drill. I guess not."

The yellow house, Roberto thought? Impossible, if it had been Eduardo who had reported Father Luis's presence there. If not – Cliff might be disguised as the priest whom Roberto had harbored – but no, he thought. Not in that so much loved house in which he no longer seemed safe or wanted. He felt himself a Panamanian, despite his mother's heritage. Warmth, yes, that he felt toward her country, for her. He couldn't remember his mother; but he had deeply loved his father and Eduardo. Even his aunt, if not to the same degree.

The telephone rang. Jimmie answered, came back to the table.

192

"It was Paula. She has come from the hospital. Laura – a severe concussion. Whether she lives – less than half a chance. Two maids from other houses were near her when she was attacked. They heard her scream – saw someone running – then saw her husband coming around the end of the wire boundary, toward her. Antonio, a bus driver."

"Antonio. God." On some mornings Roberto had ridden a bus to the University, had talked with the young driver, who once had shown him a picture of his wife Laura. Roberto remembered the pellucid hazel eyes, the delicacy of the oval face. He remembered also that Antonio had told him that both Laura and he hoped to go to the University. "If I can help you," Roberto had said. "I'm not yet on the faculty, but perhaps I will be."

Why Laura? How could she threaten the Condor? A little West Indian maid working in the Zone?

He went to the door.

"You'll come back?" Jimmie asked.

"Yes."

25
THE REVOLVER

Isabel, finding her maid too distressed that Thursday morning to be useful, released her to go to the hospital where Laura had been taken.

"I'll come back in time to get dinner, Mrs. Furniss."

"Oh, that's all right – stay if there's anything you can do."

But what a dismal start of a day, Isabel thought; Glenn off to his office before daylight – Tom in a black mood – and now housework. And of course I'm sorry about that unfortunate Laura. And Clay without a maid.

Usually, when faced with depressing problems, she telephoned Glenn, who could be depended on to cheer her. But today Glenn would be too busy to be interrupted. And Jimmie, who had never had to do housework, would not be sympathetic.

After finishing the routine work on the first floor, Isabel went upstairs. Tom's room would be the most disordered; she would

194

start there. She made the bed and began to collect the clothing scattered over the floor. Why couldn't the boy ever hang anything in the closet? In the closet, despite Celia's efforts the day before, clothes if not on the floor were half off the hangers. In moving a pile of shoes from one end, she found twelve American flags in the corner. Why would he want twelve American flags?

She put the shoes on a shelf, and started to straighten a carelessly hung jacket. On the same hanger with the jacket a belt dangled. But not an ordinary belt. It was a belt with a holster attached to it.

A game? An impersonation of a character seen on television? But Tom was too old for such games. She stared at the gun belt; then turned back into the room. Nothing in bureau drawers except rumpled clothes. The desk – the top middle drawer held a litter of pens and pencils, a pack of gum. The drawers at the right were filled with school notebooks. On the left the top drawer was locked, the lower two almost empty.

In Glenn's study downstairs the desk was similar to Tom's. Keys were in the drawer locks. One key, with a little forcing, turned the lock in the drawer in Tom's desk.

Inside the drawer were a revolver and four boxes of cartridges.

Isabel locked the drawer, kept the keys, and went downstairs again. She poured brandy.

Glenn, she thought, I must call you.

Clay answered Glenn's telephone. Glenn, he said, was at a conference with the military.

"Anything wrong, Isabel?"

"I must talk to him," Isabel said.

"I can hardly hear you – are you all right?"

She forced more volume into her voice. "I'm all right – but I *must* talk with him. Will you have him call me as soon as he comes back?"

"Yes, but I don't know –"

She lost the rest of Clay's words: the front door had opened. From the rear end of the hall she saw Tom enter and run upstairs.

Clay was still speaking.

What do I do? she thought; and realized she must have thought aloud, for Clay said impatiently, "What do you do – about what, Isabel?"

"I don't know," she said; and saw Tom running down the stairway and out through the front door.

She replaced the receiver and went upstairs.

196

The upper left desk drawer was empty, the belt and holster gone from the closet.

26
THE NEWSBOY

To Roberto's surprise – and it was the first break in the day's dark nature – Raúl García gave him an enthusiastic *abrazo* at the doorway and exclaimed, "Roberto! One of Carlos's newsboys has talked!"

Roberto returned the *abrazo*.

"What did he say?"

"Come in – I will tell you."

The lawyer ordered coffee brought to the living room.

"Carlos has just left – but what tremendous relief he left with me! The newsboy was sleeping under some news-papers on a bench in the little plaza above the marina. Early evening – but the boy was tired. And hungry. He woke when a car stopped near him. A large dark car. Three people in it. The boy thinks one of the men was Muñoz of the *Guardia* and is terrified of him. There was another man and an old woman. These two got out of the car. Not long afterward a girl came up to a small car parked near where the large one had stopped. The man and the old woman spoke to her. The boy couldn't hear what they said. He heard a clink on the concrete, when the girl dropped her car keys. The three moved away – the boy wriggled farther under the newspapers when Muñoz – if it was Muñoz – started the large car and drove away."

"Then what?" Roberto asked, setting down his coffee cup.

"Then the boy crawled out from under the papers. He was curious about the three people going toward the steps down to the marina. He followed them. In the light at the top of the steps he saw that the man was carrying the girl. The woman scolding about going down the steps – said it hurt her knees. Said she wouldn't climb up them when they came back from the island. Oh, I know – there are dozens of islands around here. But probably the one we want would be fairly near. That narrows the search. I have investigators working on all the angles I can think of."

"Good news as far as it goes," Roberto said. "Better than anything we had before. Have you heard from the kidnapers again?"

"Nothing yesterday."

"There's something I have to talk to you
198

about. Sorry to bother you now, but it's important."

García listened; and when Roberto had finished, said, "I'd been wondering about that soldier – got some of the story from Carlos. No response, I take it, to the notice about the snakeskin belt?"

"No. But Jimmie has seen snakeskin belts in a Hindu bazaar. We haven't had time to check into that angle."

"You think Cliff is safe for the moment?"

"I don't know how safe," Roberto said. "The Javanese boys – I trust them. But I don't like the temper of Chorillo. I hope you can get Cliff into U.S. Army jurisdiction."

"I can," García said. "There was a case involving a deserter once before. All the easier now, when neither side wants an incident. Though that feeling isn't unanimous here. Above all, we don't want the Condor to get hold of that boy. I'll have Tomás start to work right away. Can you get the soldier to surrender himself voluntarily?"

"He *must!* I'll see him this morning. He is afraid of everybody. Father Luis tried to persuade him to come to you. No luck. But I'll have to do it. While Tomás sees the military, the boy would be much safer here – if you'd let me bring him in."

"Yes. Careful how you do it."

"He may come disguised as a priest." Roberto smiled grimly. "I meant to ask about your wife."

"She is coming home today. Much heartened – and better after sleep in the hospital."

"I have an inquiry to make – it might help in tracking down the island," Roberto said. "I'll let you know. And if you want to call me – you can leave a message with Jimmie. We have a sort of command post at her apartment. Not the yellow house."

García nodded. Unhappily Roberto recognized comprehension in the lawyer's eyes: comprehension and grave sympathy. So García guessed – even without knowing the reasons Roberto had for questioning his brother's relations with the Condor. Miserably, he gripped García's hand and left.

On returning to the yellow house, Roberto found his aunt irritably making coffee. She wore a white and gold dressing gown; a gold ribbon firmed her black hair, long, brilliant from hours of brushing.

For once she seemed glad to see him.

"Nobody is here, Roberto. Not even Paula."

200

"Go out to the patio. I'll bring your coffee."

He finished making coffee, warmed rolls, and took a tray to his aunt.

He didn't like what he was going to do. But it was necessary.

"You don't know where Eduardo is?"

"Eduardo," his aunt said, tasting the coffee, "is inscrutable. And I worry, *chico,* because whenever I do see him, he looks so tired, so much older. Perhaps he is working too hard at the university. If you could have helped him – he counted on you."

"Yes. I am sorry. But I have been – busy."

"Perhaps busy with the niece of señor Chilton."

Let her think so, Roberto thought.

"You must know how such things go," he said. "*Tia,* I have often wondered why you did not marry again. You must have been – sought out – many times."

"The only man I would marry," Teresa said with an earnestness unlike her usual languid cynicism, "would be the man I married when I was eighteen. The husband I lost three years later. If only I had been driving with him – he drove so recklessly."

The click of her cup as she set it on the saucer ended her grieving outburst. Roberto started to reach for her hand, drew back, remembering what he had to do.

He refilled her cup, brought another roll.

The purple and white flowers breathed out a hyacinth fragrance; the sun laid diamonds in the marina waters.

"I used to think," he said, "that you rather favored Colonel Muñoz. Is he still one of your escorts?"

"Not lately. He is an animal."

How much of the epithet, Roberto wondered, was due to a genuine judgment, how much to a reaction against neglect? Even if his aunt was not captivated by Muñoz, she might resent the withdrawal of his servitude.

"Oh, I imagine – if you tolerated him – he had some good things about him."

"He had surprisingly good taste. In some ways. Small gifts. Nothing too large."

"And his island villa," Roberto said, "must have been pleasant."

Teresa shrugged. "I don't enjoy rough water and a small launch. And I had no desire to stay in that villa – he took me there once."

"Is it near Taboga? Rough water there."

"Yes. A little south of Taboga. A very small island with only a few other houses. Muñoz's house is the largest. It would be rather attractive if it were kept up. I stayed only a few minutes. An old woman was preparing dinner. Do you know, *chico*, somebody told me she was a half-sister of Muñoz – illegitimate. Much older. And he probably treats her like a slave. What a life!"

She sighed, wearily pushing a strand of hair off her forehead.

"You need a vacation," Roberto said. "Your husband's relatives in Bogotá –"

"Oh, if *only* I could go to them! I love them. But, *chico*, I have no money. Eduardo gave me some – when he got that money – was it from the coffee sale? But I needed clothes."

"I will try to arrange it," Roberto said. But how? There were the gold ornaments from Coclé – please God the golden frog would not need to be sacrificed. The breastplate – maybe that would do.

He looked with affection at the beautiful sad woman opposite him. One thing he was grateful for – she would not suffer from anything that might happen to Muñoz.

He didn't want to leave her – where the hell were Paula and the cook? Ahmad he hadn't expected, after the boy's services at Natá. That burst of action would leave Ahmad enervated for days. All right, Ahmad,

Roberto thought, just so you keep Cliff secure.

Vicky opened the door for Roberto when he went to the apartment to telephone. Jimmie had quickly bought sober dark clothing and gone out to try and see Father Luis.

Roberto telephoned García. Muñoz's retreat, he told the lawyer, was on a small island near Taboga on the south.

"Oh splendid, Roberto! The search is indeed narrowed."

"Hang in there, Raúl." And Raúl, who understood North American slang, answered. "I hang. On and on. I hire a launch – search for the island – and tonight, I think, go ashore."

"I'll go with you," Roberto said. "We can't ask Captain Reyes for help. He would sympathize – but wouldn't act against his superior in the *Guardia*. Not yet. You'll have Tomás – have you a revolver?"

"Yes. Two. And there will be four of us – you, García, Tomás, and I. God bless you, Roberto." He added, "Have you seen the soldier?"

"I am going to see him now."

How useless it was, Roberto thought, as he drove into the street on which Ahmad lived, to think anything could be stabilized for as much as a day. For the Indonesian bakery had been destroyed. Windows broken, walls charred by fire.

A car from the *Guardia* was parked in front of the smoking wreckage, two policemen looking through the rubble.

Roberto left his car near the end of the street.

"What happened?" he asked the policemen.

"The people here don't like Indonesians. It's like the trouble we had, a couple of years back, when the Chinese were driven out of their shops."

"Plenty of heat to bake his bread," the policeman said.

The place smelled, Roberto thought, as Pompeii must have smelled after the eruption.

"I must find the owner's brother – he works for me."

"Señor Villalba, no?"

"Yes. The boy Ahmad is our houseboy. I need him."

"Look at the back. They are trying to save what they can."

At the back of the shop Roberto found Ahmad, carrying a basket from which a cat protested; and Ahmad's brother Ali who was laying out water-soaked rugs and blankets in a small open area.

"Ahmad – where is Cliff?"

"Señor, I do not know." Ahmad, stricken, faced Roberto. "After the explosion he ran away. But señor, I have the priest's cat."

"Good boy. And you –" to Ahmad's brother – "I'm sorry about this."

"My whole night's baking – gone. Just gone. And everything. I don't know where we will sleep. Nothing will be safe here. But nothing is left. Fighters everywhere – what will happen, señor? Why do these people hate Indonesians?"

"God knows," Roberto said. "But you will have a place to live. You will come to my house. Both of you."

To Ahmad he said, "Which way did the soldier go? And what was he wearing?"

"He ran off to the left – he was wearing shorts we gave him and a yellow and blue shirt."

"Where do you think he went?"

"I don't know," Ahmad said. "Cantinas – what else did he know? But he had no money except those old coins."

What, Roberto thought, if he tried to find me – went to the yellow house?

"Bring whatever you can salvage," he said. "And come with me."

He installed Ahmad and Ali in the

servants' rooms under the yellow house. Before selling the golden breastplates, he drove back into Chorillo, slowly, looking for Cliff, and finally finding him hidden behind a newspaper in a dingy cantina in Chorillo. Immeasurably relieved, he seated himself on a stool beside the soldier.

"Keep your old coins, boy," he said. "I'll pay for our drinks. I need to talk to you."

"The cat," Cliff said. "I had to leave him."

"The cat is all right," Roberto said. "He's at my house. With the Indonesian boys."

"That priest – such a decent guy," Cliff said. "I didn't want to lose his cat. And the Indonesians were decent – what goes on here?"

"They're building up – toward riots," Roberto said. "Listen to me, Cliff."

Cliff listened. But it took Roberto almost two hours to persuade the boy to give himself up to the lawyer.

Since García's house might well be under surveillance by the Condor, an immediate problem – but weren't all the problems he faced immediate? – was to deliver Cliff safely without recognition. Ahmad and his brother in addition to providing shorts and shirt and sandals, had given Cliff dark glasses and a drooping Panama hat. Fortunately, the boy had kept the deep tan acquired from his Army training, so that he did not seem conspicuously different from a Panamanian youth – unless he spoke.

"I know," Roberto said, "how we'll get you into the lawyer's house. Wait while I telephone." He came back a few minutes later. "This time, Cliff, you won't have to be a priest."

"I like being a priest."

"We would have to give you a tonsure if you kept on being a priest. No. This will be simpler. You are now the boy friend of Elena, one of the García maids. She will be looking for you. You'll go to the back door; when Elena comes out, you'll kiss her. Make it look real, but don't say anything. Let Elena do the talking."

"What's she going to say?"

"Oh – that she is glad to see you – wants you to come in. There will probably be another maid there – she may kiss you too."

Cliff rubbed his chin. "I haven't shaved."

"You look all right," Roberto assured him. "I'll give you candy to take to the maids. The Garcías are wonderful people. Just do whatever señor García tells you to do."

"What happens if the maid's real boy friend turns up?"

"No worry. Elena will have told him about you. The main thing is to get you into the house so that any watcher won't be suspicious. But be sure not to speak until you are inside."

"What if somebody else comes to the back door? What if I kiss the wrong person?"

"You won't. Elena will come to the door."

The bartender sent one of the omnipresent tip-seeking boys to buy candy; he returned with two gaudy boxes done up in crimson and purple ribbons.

"Is she pretty?" Cliff asked dubiously.

"Very pretty. A West Indian."

Roberto drove Cliff to within two blocks of the lawyer's house, told him exactly how to go the rest of the way, and then returned to Chorillo to look for the warehouse where Ahmad had told him the boys' club had their headquarters. The only boys he found were twenty or thirty sweating, lean men, less shaven than Cliff, practicing a drill with wooden clubs instead of arms. He thought they would have no use for roller skates.

His visit to a jeweler was more productive: the golden breastplate brought a comfortable surplus over the cost of air fare to Bogotá.

"Can you be ready to leave this afternoon?" he asked his aunt on returning to the yellow house. He found her more cheerful than she had been in the morning: Ali had cooked an excellent East Indian curry for lunch; Paula had reappeared; even the cook had come, but had angrily taken off, after encountering Indonesians in the kitchen.

"Of course I will be ready!" Teresa said.

"I have telephoned for your reservation." He gave her an envelope. "This is for your ticket – a little more. And I'll try to send you what you might need. I will drive you to Tocumen."

"Thank you, Roberto."

She kissed him, held his shoulders, searched his eyes.

"Something is wrong, *chico?* Is it with Eduardo?"

"If it is, I will do what I can."

"Your eyes, *chico* – they look unhappy.

"It's because they are near-sighted, *tía.* "

She shook her head. "I don't think so. If by staying here I could help in any way –"

"No, *mi tía.* It would help us both if you were safe in Bogotá."

He found himself returning to memories, induced perhaps by his aunt's unusual warmth. She had known Toto, the sheepdog, in the years following – so quickly – the death of Roberto's mother from pneumonia, the

210

death of Teresa's husband, the death of Roberto's father – those few years in which the three – Teresa, Eduardo, Roberto himself, had been close. Eduardo had been shocked by Roberto's attempt to barber Toto's hair into a Hapsburg beard. It had been Teresa who had defended the four-year old Roberto – not that Eduardo would have been harsh – but Teresa had gathered Roberto into her arms, shielding him against Eduardo's punitive impulses.

"*Tía,*" he said now, "do you remember Toto?"

"Our sheep dog? Of course. He had been your mother's – but we all adored him. It was hard, though, to guess what he was thinking – under all that hair. I wish we had him now. A sweet dog. Oh, Roberto, I wish we could have another sheep dog."

Roberto stopped the question in his mind: will I ever see her again? Stopped the question, tinged with fatality – will Eduardo and I come out of what is to happen?

He gave orders to the Indonesians for his aunt's dinner, told Paula, wandering like a ghost with a dust-brush through the rooms, to go home or to the hospital where Laura still lay unconscious, guarded by her husband and a policeman.

After taking his aunt to the airport, he

went to Jimmie's apartment, found her in a too-large black skirt and blouse, a masquerading child, but not with a child's face. She looked emaciated, pale, harassed.

"Roberto, Eduardo blew my cover. I sent a message – to ask to see padre Luis – saying I was a cousin – talked to a young kind of intern-looking boy – the whole place seemed like a hospital. Priests everywhere – talking different brands of Spanish. Before my intern came back, Eduardo came out – I think from Father Sebastian's lair – saw me – Roberto, he looks so tired – so much older – and another intern came out, said Father Sebastian wanted to see me – but Eduardo stopped him. He said, no need. This girl is not a cousin. An imposter. Then Eduardo took me by the arm – hard grip – took me out to my car. 'Go home, Jimmie. And stay there,' he said. Oh, damn, Roberto – I could at least have told Father Luis that his cat is all right."

"Well, you tried, Jimmie."

He told her what had happened during the morning.

"You'll go to the island tonight? Oh I wish I could help."

"You help by staying here. When we need to telephone. Where is Vicky?"

212

"Marketing. She should be back within an hour."

"I don't," Roberto said, "want you to be alone. Would you mind if I sent Ahmad over here to stay with you?"

"No," Jimmie said. "And what are you going to do? Any chance you could come back this afternoon or tonight?"

"Nothing I'd like better," Roberto said. "But today – I don't know. I do need to use your telephone."

If Jimmie wondered why he couldn't telephone from the yellow house, she did not question him. First he called Ahmad, who said he would come to the apartment in minutes. Next Roberto called García: yes, Cliff had arrived, been accepted by the maid, was safe.

Something settled – for how long?

27
DESIGNS OF THE CONDOR

Thursday night. The meeting place for the Condor was damp from long afternoon showers.

"We haven't had time," the priest said to

Eduardo, "to familiarize you with some of our operative principles. We use no names in our conferences. We ask each other no questions. But." He shot a glance at Muñoz on his right. "We do *not* take any important unilateral action. And if such action should be *absolutely* necessary, we report it."

Muñoz dropped a sodden cigar butt on the stone floor and stepped on it.

"Why address me?" he asked. "I would have said the same thing to you."

Dissension? Eduardo wondered. Distrust? Had the old politician, now dead and buried, held the other two together by his peculiar endowments of cajolery and threat? By his sinister charisma? And will my role be to serve as scapegoat if the other two men find themselves hard-pressed.

Each of the two seemed to be blaming the other for unilateral action – unless one was acting, or unless neither had taken such action. What action? Chilton's murder? And possibly the attack on the maid Laura? And if neither of these two men was responsible for Chilton's death, who was? He reviewed the night of Chilton's murder. From nine until a little after two he had been at a party at the Union Club. After the short drive home, he had been with his aunt and Roberto until they had gone to bed. Their answers to Captain Reyes's questioning had agreed with his. Both had been indefinite about the time between leaving Eduardo on the terrace and hearing him call for help from the marina.

The priest was speaking to Eduardo again.

"Before we discuss our urgent business, I must say that it was unfortunate that you were seen this morning near my office and by that girl, the niece. I understand she had come to see the trouble-making priest, pretending to be a relative. What did you do about her?"

"Took her to her car and told her to go home and stay there."

"Was that masquerade her idea or your brother's?"

"I assume," Eduardo said, "that she felt responsible for the priest's difficulties – because of that prayer at her uncle's grave."

"We do not make assumptions," the older man said harshly. "When did you learn about the prayer?"

"Our colleague –" Eduardo gestured toward Muñoz – "had a representative at the burial."

Muñoz nodded. His attitude, Eduardo noticed, was less hostile than that of Father Sebastian. The beginning of a new alignment? One to be wary of, he thought.

"One more question. When will the ship return?"

"I have made contact with the crew at the usual port. Verbally, but in code, of course. Repairs have been made, cargo is being loaded. The ship should be here Saturday or Sunday. If they run into delay in transiting the Canal, they have orders to anchor off Colon and let me know."

Father Sebastian nodded. "Awkward timing. However." He laid three maps of Panama City on the table. "Now I ask for your thorough concentration."

Before distributing the maps, he said to Eduardo, "I want you to produce copy for another sheet similar to these. By tomorrow morning. I will have them copied for distribution."

The first sheet was topped by a drawing of a condor. The headline read: *"El cóndor – el corazón de su país."* Below, continuing in Spanish, the script read:

Who is this Condor? Soon you will know him – will know his plans for your welfare, your prosperity, your freedom from the menace of oppression.

The second sheet read:

Friends, Panamanians:
Your Condor knows that you are unhappy about the Treaties that the United States is choking down our parched throats. The second Treaty has now been passed. The Condor knows, as you do, that the Treaties give us too little and too slowly. You must watch for the announcement of a rally in the Grand Plaza. Be on guard, Citizens of Panama!

Eduardo read the announcements, firming his face against expression. El Cóndor – the heart of the country! As if, he thought, the Condor had heart for anything except the coup that would bring power. He noticed that the announcements were loosely enough worded so that they would appeal to dissident leftist as well as nationalist groups.

"What facet of our plans," he asked, "do you want the third sheet to announce?"

"Denunciation of control by the United States – of our present government's policies. Removal of the pestilential Canal Zone. Castigation of the unfair system of letting only North Americans use the Commissaries."

Eduardo refrained from pointing out that

217

removal of the Canal Zone would also remove the Commissaries. But how reason with these people?

"Now here are copies of the map which the Colonel and I have prepared. His objectives are marked in green; yours, Eduardo, in red – you will see that you will be responsible for the seizure of radio and television stations. The point of distribution for all materials will be the old warehouse in Chorillo, which is ringed in black. My post will be in our helicopter with two-way radio communication; both of you will have similar equipment, as will six of our subordinates stationed at strategic places and mobile, so that control can be strengthened when necessary. The action will start at noon on Saturday when Colonel Muñoz takes possession of the *Presidencia* and other government buildings and the *Guardia* headquarters. Simultaneously the guerrillas will be unleashed from the Chorillo district."

"And at the radio and television stations," Eduardo said, "what help do I have?"

"You will be supported by insurgents from Chorillo directed by a member of the *Guardia*. They will come to their posts at noon. I assign the communications points to you because you will announce the take-over in authoritative language. Also the take-over of the government buildings."

Dios, Eduardo thought. The *Presidencia* to be taken over – so near the yellow house.

"Have you other questions?" the priest asked coldly.

"No, your Eminence."

"You anticipate," Father Sebastian said, smiling.

So, Eduardo thought, the red hat of a cardinal was Father Sebastian's goal. And Muñoz's goal? He was risking a good deal – and for what? A place on a *junta* – if this plan succeeded? Rewards more material than prestigious? Or was Muñoz counting on an effacement of the priest and his own elevation to headship of the nation? Eduardo had no illusions about his own relations with these other two. If either needed a scapegoat, he would be chosen. In an interim, his name, whatever influence he had among intellectuals – oh yes, these attributes would be used. *Dios* – if only he could take the *Isla* – and his family – and escape.

Again he wondered about Muñoz, study-ing the man's heavy but not altogether unattractive features. Brutish? perhaps. But that was preferable to the gray ice-cold of the priest's eyes, the compressed lips, the emanations of monstrous egotism and potential cruelty. The priest, he thought, should have lived in fifteenth-century Spain, not in the twentieth century in this hemisphere.

"Have you any more questions?" the priest asked.

"Two," Eduardo said. "In announcements I am to make, should there be allusions to our policy toward foreigners? A policy of excluding or removing them would, as you probably realize, alienate our support from leftist groups."

"We will make no statement about foreigners for the moment," the priest said.

"Another question. You have undoubtedly provided for the possibility that your helicopter might be attacked?"

"Yes. We have another helicopter, another pilot in reserve. But there will be no threat. The action should be completed before the United States Army could decide to intervene – which is not likely anyway. And if there is any threat from them, they will be notified that my helicopter carries a bomb which will be dropped on one of the Canal locks."

28
DEVIL MASKS

The dark sea was another sky, starred with phosphorescence which shifted constellation patterns in the rise and fall of waves, but a sky near enough to be sensed in the spray that washed over the deck of the launch and in the salt scent breathed by the four men on board.

Any lights on the islet they were approaching were obscured by dense jungle trees; but lights on a few small boats at the eastern end guided them toward the shore, where they made out a fragile-looking dock. When the launch was moored at the dock, its riding light briefly showed red devils' masks on the four men who ascended the flimsy steps and went ashore.

Roberto, in the lead, carried a shielded flashlight. Four houses beside the largest one, for which they were looking; that was what Teresa had said. They found two cottages near the water; then, farther along the shore, a larger one; beyond it two more small structures. The large one, then, was the one they wanted.

Silently the four men began to circle the house. In a room at the rear a light shone; radio music sounded. From the shelter of a palm, they saw an old woman reaching up to close a door in a kitchen cabinet, and beyond her a man at a table lighting a pipe. At the front of the house a thin and dim light outlined a window and shone through a small opening – a knothole in a board that covered the window?

The radio music from the kitchen stopped. Roberto, after a whisper to Tomás, went back to the tree shelter at the rear, where he heard a radio announcement. He heard something else, the barking of a dog, and saw the man with the pipe get up and move out of sight toward the front of the house. Roberto was rounding the back of the building when a door at the front opened and a doberman ran through the rectangle of light toward the end of the house where Roberto stood, now gripping a revolver by the barrel. As the dog sprang, Robert clubbed its head with the revolver butt, then as the animal fell, crouched beside it. He heard the footsteps of the man approaching from the doorway. Beyond the rectangle of light, the man halted, peered into the darkness, called to the dog, then muttered, "Crazy beast," and turned back. At the sound of Roberto's whistled signal to the others, the man halted again abruptly. In the moment that he stood there within a few feet of the door, all four men had surrounded him. He saw the red devils' masks, the drawn revolvers, shouted once, then fell as Tomás struck him. Roberto snatched from a pocket the scarf he had brought to use as a gag. Tomás pulled off the coil of rope he wore around his neck. They heard the stumbling steps of the old woman in the hallway, heard her horrified screams as the other two devil-masked men seized her. San Martín pushed her into a chair in the kitchen and bound her. García was already running down the hall toward the room with the boarded window. He found the key in the lock.

Roberto heard him call "Graciela!" as he opened the door, heard Graciela cry out first in terror, then – and he would not soon forget the rapture in her words: "Papá – it is you!"

He heard García, clamping down emotion, say, "Who did you think it was – a devil? Put something on – God, what a nasty lace thing you're wearing." They came into the hall, Graciela in a black dressing gown, her father carrying a blanket.

"On to the boat," San Martín said

happily. And Tomás, hailing the rescue, said, "No shoes? I'll carry her?"

"You will not. I carry my child," García said.

"Are they all devils?" Garciela said. As her father carried her to the dock, she added, "From now on I am a devil worshiper."

Roberto pulled off his mask.

"Don't let me stop you," he said.

Across the water the suffused luminescence ahead of them firmed and separated into the lights of the buildings of Panama City.

"No," Graciela said, answering questions, "they didn't hurt me. Drugs – yes, at first. But the old woman was kind. They told me – that first night – that you, Papá, had sent for me – then there was a drug. A needle prick. I woke up in that house. I hope you didn't have to hurt the old woman?"

"No," San Martín said. "I tied her loosely – couldn't bear to gag her. Anyway, I don't think people in the nearest house would hear her. Of course – they'll get loose – telephone – but by then you'll be safe, Graci. Home. And we'll be guarding the house."

"I think," García said, "that we can count on help from Captain Reyes."

They sank the devil masks, which had come from a shop that sold carnival supplies, in the sea before they reached the marina. It had been San Martín's idea to use them, and he seemed sorry to abandon them.

29
EXPLOSION

At breakfast on Friday Roberto was surprised when Eduardo joined him.

"Where is our aunt? She wasn't here when I came home last night and isn't here now."

Roberto explained.

"A good idea," his brother said. "In fact, I had been thinking of the same thing. And meaning to give her money for the trip. How did she manage?"

"I arranged it."

"*You* did? I've been meaning to give you money, too. The servants – by the way, do we have a new cook? We've never had fresh pastry for breakfast."

"Ahmad's brother," Roberto said. "He had a bakery – lost everything in a fire yesterday. So I took him on. Our previous cook didn't like finding Indonesians in the kitchen and left. Just as well. She hardly ever cooked. I don't know why we kept her as long as we did."

"Our aunt liked her. And speaking of our aunt – she went off without saying good-bye to me."

"She asked me to say it for her."

"I wished you could have gone with her," Eduardo said. "At lest for a week or two. Go now?"

Roberto shook his head. "Too busy. I have to finish the work for my master's by the end of the semester. Also two courses and a thesis seminar for the doctorate."

Eduardo looked puzzled as though the University belonged to a region of fantasy. As Roberto had foreseen, he had forgotten his promise to meet his classes. On Roberto's desk now forty term papers lay waiting to be read.

"What about final examinations, Eduardo?"

"Finals? You give them. Or better, we will omit finals."

Roberto was about to protest that even if examinations were omitted, grades would have to be made out for eighty some students, but he was checked by the weariness in his brother's face and by Eduardo's sudden turning toward him and saying without his usual half-patronizing, half-affectionate banter, "Thank you, Roberto."

Urgently for a moment Roberto longed to tell Eduardo what he, Roberto, was to do today. Impossible, he knew; equally impossible to deviate from what he had to do.

By ten-thirty Roberto had made two telephone calls. The first was to García, who told him that Graciela was well and that Cliff, having made a deposition, would be transferred safely within the hour to the Army base in the Canal Zone. The snakeskin belt and the coins García was keeping as evidence in a trial. And at noon the lawyer and Tomás would destroy Chilton's papers.

"An incredible relief – to be able to carry out a friend's wishes – although the loss, the waste, of so much of his work is appalling."

"Yes," Roberto said. "A man with less moral sinew than you, señor, would have capitulated. And Graciela is safe."

"Safe," her father said. "But I am not allowing her to leave the house. Not at present. And I have three trusted men on duty as guards. Four, if you count the loyal Tomás. There will, I think, be an announcement of an engagement soon. I couldn't have hoped for anything happier – for Graci and for my wife and me."

"And for Tomás," Roberto said. "Does Jimmie know?"

"Graci will telephone her today. These children –" he laughed. "They are so impulsive. Graci has already talked to me about the wedding. And I believe my wife has been designing a wedding gown. Do you know, Roberto, I could not be fonder of Tomás if he were my son?"

That avenue of happiness gave some warmth to Roberto's day.

His second telephone call was to San Martín, whose friend Diego Campos, a contractor, was to help Roberto. Happiness? None from this call, but assurance that he would have support from a man who knew how to accomplish what had to be done. Diego, San Martín said, was already on his way to the yellow house.

"Let me go with you, Roberto. What a story it will make!"

"No. Whatever story – it will be yours. But you have done enough. You must not be involved in anything that might have legal complications. If the wrong side comes out on top."

Roberto heard San Martín mutter something about the impossibility of the wrong side's victory. I hope to God he is right, Roberto thought.

He went out to the parking area, where Diego's gray panel truck stood in the space usually occupied by Eduardo's car. There was no driver in the truck; but in front of the apartment house, where the slight Javanese were struggling to move the cartons of roller skates, Roberto saw a tall and sturdy man easily load a carton on a wheelbarrow, then the second. He went toward the man.

"Diego?"

"Yes. Roberto?"

"Thank you for your help."

Ahmad and Ali were wheeling the barrow toward the yellow house, where the cartons were to be stored in the lower court.

"We'll be going – as soon as you are ready," Diego said, moving toward his truck. "I have hard hats for us. Gauntlets. Goggles. The other things we'll need. Canteens of water. But you'll have to bring boots. And a shirt with sleeves. This won't be a picnic."

Roberto found a jacket and riding boots – unused for how long? How I would like to see Jimmie, he thought. But no time now. In the kitchen Ali had prepared sandwiches and a gallon thermos jug of lemonade. "Señor," he said, "I am not asking what you are going to do. But I wish I could help you."

Ahmad rose from where he had been

kneeling under a cabinet to feed Negrito, said, "Señor – what *can* we do?"

"Stay here," Roberto said. "And yes, Ali – please go over to Miss Jimmie's apartment and tell her to stay there. Not to go out. I will try to see her later. And if Paula comes, don't let her go home alone. The city – well, you know."

"Yes," Ali said. "We have seen riots before. Here, señor, I will help you carry these things outside."

Diego loaded into the truck what they had brought, took his place behind the wheel, and when Roberto had seated himself, started the truck.

"On our way," he said stoutly.

"I can't," Roberto said as they drove through the dense traffic on the Avenida Central, where posters and painted signs on walls extolled the valor and idealism of the Condor, "tell you what your help means to me."

Diego shrugged. "After what San Martín told me, what else could I do? My work is to erect buildings, not to see them destroyed."

As they approached the International Bridge, a sudden torrent of rain drowned the windshield despite the labor of the wipers. Through the wall of water Roberto made out

230

the shape of two United States cruisers at anchor in the roadstead beyond Balboa. Within ten minutes after the truck had crossed the bridge, the rain stopped and the sun blazed through the intensified humidity.

"Better to get the rain out of the way now than later," Diego said.

His solidity and conviction helped Roberto to feel the substantiality of what otherwise would have seemed an almost visionary attempt. But he still had misgivings.

"I hope San Martín warned you that if the wrong people come out on top, you could have trouble."

"If the wrong people win I'd be in trouble anyway. I've too many associates marked as leftists. Though for the present the Condor is appealing to both sides. My son – at the University – runs with the leftist pack. Ready to riot. I've told him that a Condor regime would – in the end – be viciously rightist. And what does the boy say? Only that any change would be better than no change. Change. Ferment. He has his placards ready. Weapons? I hope not. But he and a lot of other students will be out with the insurgents tomorrow. Unless what you and I will do today stops them short. You are a student. What do you think about right and left?"

"If I had to choose between a rightist tyranny and a leftist I would choose the leftist," Roberto said. "But not by taking part in rioting. Leftist – rightist – the terms don't mean very much. Intentions do – and some degree of humanization. Is that the word?"

"As good as any other," Diego said. "You're younger than I thought you'd be. San Martín thinks a lot of you. Look at that." He pointed to a Condor sign painted on the white wall of a house in the village through which they were passing. The rain had washed the red ink of the lettering into anemic blood-colored rivulets. He glanced at Roberto, pounded his left thigh. "You've got courage – now look up. You aren't alone against these sons of bitches. A couple of hours and we'll have done what we can and be out of all this."

Yes, Roberto thought. And Eduardo? What about him? What would happen to Eduardo if his brother thwarted the Condor plans? Oh, if only Eduardo had nothing to do with the Condor – if Eduardo at this moment could be, as in the past, diverting himself – with a woman – in a game of tennis – with anything except the sordid pursuits of the Condor.

Diego stopped the truck. On their left the

jungle spilled into the road: scarlet passion flowers, emerald vine-covered trees, trees bearing violet orchids.

Roberto felt Diego's eyes fixed on his clenched fists.

Diego handed him the key to the rear of the truck.

"You need food. You brought some. So did I. Get out. Unlock the rear door. Do you think I don't know what boys look like when they are hungry?"

Roberto unlocked the hack door of the truck, took out sandwiches. "Please have some."

Diego shook his head. "I eat breakfast. A steak, sausages, fried eggs. A large breakfast. Not like the skimped things you children eat. What did you have for breakfast?"

"I don't remember."

"No wonder. Not with what you had ahead." He started the truck.

They drove between the jungle walls in the scalding heat until they sighted the broken columns and the crownless arches of the ancient Indian city. Diego parked the truck near the wall.

"A new wall. A thirty-mile wind would level it. The Coclé Indians would have done better."

Near where they had stopped two laundry

trucks were parked...Ironic, Roberto thought. Laundry trucks at Coclé where the Indians had worn no clothes, only ornaments.

No truck drivers were in sight.

"Probably taking a *siesta* out there under the palms," Diego said.

Roberto looked inside the trucks. One was partly loaded, the other without cargo. The ignition keys were in the locks. An empty wine bottle lay on the ground between the trucks.

"In this heat they'll be sleeping soundly," Diego said. "But not heavily enough."

"Immobilize them?" Roberto said. "In the empty truck? Drive it out to the road?"

Diego nodded. "They may be armed." From his truck he brought rope and two revolvers, one of which he gave to Roberto; the rope he looped over the opened rear door of the truck.

The two drivers, wearing khaki shorts and sandals, lay asleep under the palms. From the belt of one man a revolver butt showed.

Holding his own revolver in his right hand, Diego withdrew the driver's revolver with his left hand. The man awoke with a cry which aroused his partner.

"On your feet," Diego ordered. "Both of you. Walk to the empty truck."

When they reached the truck, he forced the two men to lie down at the left of the door, then placed his revolver inside his belt. Roberto covered the drivers with his revolver while Diego roped them together. He kept to their right, so that Roberto's coverage would be unobstructed.

"Who are you?" the driver who had lost his weapon muttered.

"Not the Condor," Diego said.

"The Condor will slice you into shreds – send your souls to hell!" the other driver cried.

"Where he will be ahead of us," Diego said grimly. He closed the rear door of the truck. "All right, Roberto. Drive these bastards down close to the road."

Earlier in the day, after Ali had delivered Roberto's message, Jimmie, disappointed at not seeing Roberto, returned to what she had been doing for the past two hours – studying her uncle's cryptic notes on the pad that she had kept from that dreadful Monday morning. Vicky, who rarely complained about anything, and never about what affected herself, came frowning into the study.

"I need to go to the market. What are we going to have for dinner? It's Friday and I

235

wanted to get a nice fish – maybe shrimps. There ought to be a lot of good choices today. Do you think it's all as dangerous as Mr. Roberto said? If I went out now, I could be back in an hour or so."

"Don't go," Jimmie said. "Roberto knows what he is talking about. Damn. I wish I knew where he was. What he's up to."

"You can be sure he'll come as soon as he can. Did Ali tell you anything?"

"No. But he didn't look very cheerful. He just said that Roberto had gone out with a man in a truck. He didn't know where they were going."

"About dinner," Vicky said.

"There must be something here – a canned ham?"

"Yes. I could make a fruit glaze and a chocolate pie."

"Keep it simple," Jimmie said. "Look at what we had for breakfast – that super omelet – baked *platanos* – and an egg not for me at ten. I'll founder."

"You need it. You're too thin," Vicky said. "And we have no sherry."

"Never mind. I'll drink Scotch."

"Well," Vicky said, won over, "all right then. But if riots tear everything up tomorrow –"

"If they do," Jimmie said, "we'll live on canned soup and cheese."

Vicky shuddered. She stooped to caress the ivory Frangi, who slept elongated in an air-swept channel near the terrace door.

Jimmie stood up. "I'm not getting anywhere," she said. "I've got to do something. I suppose the police have questioned the people in the other two apartments here – about last Sunday night."

"The police," Vicky said scornfully. "Who knows what they have done? You could try. The people in the apartment under us are a man in the U.S. Embassy and his wife, but they're on vacation in the States. Over us there's the family with the yellow cat."

"I'll go there," Jimmie said.

The door to the third-floor apartment was opened by a tall young blonde.

"I'm Jimmie Chilton. May I talk to you for a few minutes?"

"Of course – come in, Miss Chilton. I've been meaning to see you – we're so terribly sorry about your uncle."

A pretty but mutinous-looking child, a girl of about ten, came to inspect the visitor.

"Forgive the mess here," her mother said. She pointed to a vacuum cleaner supine on the living room floor. "My husband has an

237

agency to sell these wretched things – but if confronted in the flesh I don't suppose he'd know how to fix this one. The damn thing won't run with the handle up – what am I supposed to do – crawl?"

"Wish I could help," Jimmie said. "But everywhere looks clean anyway."

"It isn't. Cake crumbs – cat fur – the maid didn't come – can't blame her – the streets are not safe. My husband called from his office. He told me not to let Clorinda go to school. Please sit down. Can I give you something cool to drink?"

"Thanks, no. I just wanted to ask you – I don't know whether the *Guardia* have questioned you – but did anyone here hear anything unusual last Sunday night? Over the marina?"

"The *Guardia* questioned us. But our bedrooms are at the front and side of the building. We didn't hear anything."

"I wasn't in my room," Clorinda said. "Too hot. I came out to the sofa in the living room."

"You didn't tell us," her mother said.

"I didn't like the man from the *Guardia*."

"You're sure it was Sunday night?" her mother asked.

"Yes. That was the night Daddy had to

drive a man to the airport. It rained. I heard Daddy come in. It was hot after the rain; so I went out to the sofa. Next thing I knew, the kitten woke me, chasing something over the floor. I put her out on the terrace and came back inside. Then I heard the vines rustling. Below our terrace. I thought somebody was climbing up. Scary. But nothing happened up here. I got a chocolate bar out of the refrigerator and ate it. It was cooler, and I was starting to go back to my room when I heard an awfully big splash in the marina. I was terrified it might be the kitten, but she was scratching at the screen door."

Jimmie shivered. Immediate, painful was the meaning of the child's story: the murderer returning, climbing up the stout vines to the second-floor terrace, then lowering or dropping the poor body into the marina.

Clorinda's mother, pale, frightened, put her arms around her daughter. "Clorrie – you didn't go out on the terrace – no one saw you?"

"No. I let the kitten in and went to bed. Why? Should I have gone out to look?"

"No!"

Jimmie stood up. "Thank you, Clorinda. You've been a big help."

"I suppose," the mother said, as Jimmie

went to the door, "I should tell the *Guardia* about this."

"I think so," Jimmie said.

When she went down to her apartment, she found a handbill under the door, a sheet showing a crude representation of a condor with a Panamanian flat in its beak and the heading: *"El Condor – Corazón de su país! Recuerde el sabado!"*

Heart of your country – what a dark arrogant claim. And "Remember Saturday." That would be tomorrow.

She showed the sheet to Victoria, who scowled at it.

"Will those people wait until tomorrow? I turned on the television while you were gone. *Avenida Central* choked with people – sticks, stones being thrown. Mr. Roberto was right. Better to stay indoors. Stores closed. Grilles lowered. Did you find out anything?"

Jimmie told her; then, remembering, wept.

"That child – that little girl – so near the horror –"

"*Nina,*" Victoria said, "don't cry. The child is safe. She couldn't have been seen. And think of this: your friend Graciela – she is at home. Out of danger."

"Thank heaven!" Jimmie wiped her eyes.

"When she called this morning, she was – almost gay. She wanted to come here, but her father wouldn't let her."

She looked out of a window and saw Roberto's car still parked outside the yellow house.

The day's rain was starting as she brought the pad with her uncle's last notes to the living-room table, dense rain that closed her and Victoria into an apartment isolated from any other part of the world. Victoria was setting dough for rolls into pans for the second rising. The cat Frangi jumped up to the table and was not reprimanded.

Jimmie tried new approaches to the notes, reading them aloud, as someone had told her Chaucer should be read, for the associations of sound; trying also to hear the notes in Spanish. "Man of the River," she read aloud and in Spanish. "The angler who escaped." "Of the River – del Rio." Del Rio – the border town in Texas, which she remembered her uncle had mentioned, from the early years of his work as crime reporter? An escaped angler – someone named Fisher? Another word, read aloud now, made her remember a conversation with her uncle. Was that word connected somehow with Del Rio? A thin small chance. But she started a long distance call to the Chief of Police in Del Rio, Texas.

Before the international operator could complete the connection, Isabel called, an almost hysterical Isabel, to tell Jimmie that Glenn was sending Tom to cousins in Virginia, that Tom was to leave today, and to be put into a military academy.

"But why, Isabel?"

"Because the wretched boy had got a gun – and was carrying it around with him. Anger about the treaties – that is one thing – but a gun – right now – with Glenn trying to keep the situation cool here – and not easy –"

"How did Tom get the gun?"

"He won't tell. He keeps saying, 'I'm not a rat.'"

"Slow down, Isabel. Maybe it's what Tom needs – a stiffer school."

"But he will feel exiled," Isabel said. "Not that I don't – in a way – envy him – how I would love to get away from here. Before the natives take over. If I got a gun –" her voice rose – "do you suppose Glenn might send me to the States?"

"Stop it. You wouldn't leave Glenn. You know that."

Isabel was crying.

"Look, Isabel. You've had plenty of difficulty with Tom. Why for God's sake don't you accept this – make your life with Glenn as easy as you can – no friction over the boy – and remember, this is harder for Glenn than for you."

Isabel was silent for a moment, then laughed.

"You crazy kid," she said. "You sound as if you were a hundred years old."

"I am. So go to Tocumen with them. Don't magnify the importance."

"Tom's going to fly on a military jet on mission to the States. Glenn doesn't want to risk Panama – things too uneasy. Jimmie – you'd be safer with us."

"I'll be all right," Jimmie said. The international operator broke in to say that Del Rio, Texas was on the line.

Isabel hung up; and Jimmie heard the warm drawl of the Police Chief in Del Rio. No, he said, he had been Chief only eight years – but the old man – who had been Chief in the '40s – maybe he'd remember something, and meanwhile there were records – could they call back?

"Call back collect," Jimmie said.

She did some pacing through the room until Vicky, quiet, soothing, opened the door to the terrace.

"Sit down out here, Miss Jimmie. I found some port wine – will you have some?"

"No, thanks."

Within an hour the return call came from Texas. And when Jimmie had taken it, she dialed a local number.

A few minutes later she made for the door.

"I'm going to Laura – to stay with her until her husband comes. The nurse at the desk says the police guard has been called away. Vicky, do you know what time Antonio gets off work?"

"Around five," Vicky said. "Please don't drive – the traffic is bad. And people are beginning to hold up signs telling yanquis to go home."

Jimmie looked down at the street through one of the windows in what had been her uncle's study.

"No," she said to Victoria. "I couldn't get a taxi in that welter. And other streets may be worse. I'll take a chance with my car."

"I'd like to go with you."

"Thank you, Vicky – but there may be phone calls. If Roberto calls or comes here, please tell him I had to go – to stay with Laura until her husband gets there."

"Yes, I understand. But I don't feel very good about seeing you go out into the city. Alone. My nephew called while you were in the apartment upstairs. He said the city was like a volcano getting ready to erupt. There hadn't been any shooting – that would come tomorrow – but the rabble weren't waiting for the Condor's signals."

"You'd better stay here tonight," Jimmie said.

"Yes," Vicky said. "I told my nephew not to come for me. I don't want you to be here alone."

Jimmie hugged her.

"I'll be back – it should be a little after five. Don't worry, Vicky."

From the street entrance Jimmie saw in front of the *Presidencia* banks of men from the *Guardia* and a stream of insurgents with their placards. The police were not halting them. In the parking area outside the yellow house Roberto's car still stood. Where, she wondered as she pushed toward her car, parked near the plaza, were all these people on normal days?

Please God I won't be too late, Jimmie thought as she drove at scarcely more than walking speed through streets clogged with men and women and bristling with Condor signs. The small square in front of the hospital held no promise of parking; she had to leave her car three blocks away in an alley. From there she ran to the hospital. At the desk on the main floor a nurse faced a switchboard; she turned, haggard-faced, toward Jimmie.

"I must see Laura. The West Indian girl."

"Yes. The one who had the guard – but he went out hours ago – you saw what the square is like. And almost everybody else has gone out. Two bloody accidents in the square." She tore at her ebony smooth hair. "Patients need help – I've tried – there doesn't seem to be anybody else here – except me and the patients. Laura is on the third floor – room 327."

"Nobody has come in to see her?"

"Nobody I've seen – but somebody could have got by the desk while I was busy at the switchboard. I'm glad you came – see what you can do for Laura. The elevator isn't running – use the stairs back here at the right."

On the third floor Jimmie ran through empty corridors and found room 327, where Laura under a halo of bandages lay looking like a Byzantine madonna. A second bed in the room was unoccupied. Laura opened her eyes and showed recognition when Jimmie spoke.

"Laura – dear. Is there anything I can do for you?"

"Antonio?" Laura whispered.

"He has probably been held up in the traffic. I thought I would stay with you until he came. Are you hungry? Thirsty?"

"A little hungry," Laura said. "It must be that I am better."

"Dear good girl! I will find something for you – I'm so glad you feel better." So glad, Jimmie thought, that you are safe. "There must be a pantry on this floor. I'll be back in a few minutes."

Laura smiled. "Thank you, Miss Jimmie. Would you close the window? So much noise outside."

Jimmie shut the window, noticing the narrow balcony outside. Below, the small plaza was crowded with people and cars. She saw two ambulances about a block from the hospital.

Around a turn in the corridor she found a pantry with a refrigerator in which there were containers of milk and of eggs. She considered making Laura an eggnog but decided against it because she did not want to leave Laura for more than the promised few minutes. She filled a glass with milk and a plate with biscuits from a box on a counter, put glass and plate on a tray and started back toward Laura's room.

The few minutes had been too long.

From the doorway she saw a man pull a

247

pillow from the unoccupied bed: a tall agile man, his face hidden from her. A moment's hope that he was Antonio died as the man pushed the pillow over Laura's face.

Jimmie threw the tray at him, shouting for help.

Releasing his pressure on the pillow, the man sprang toward her.

It was Clay Austin.

He seized her arms and pulled her around the foot of the bed. Jimmie kicked him, heard him gasp with pain. Before she could kick again, he freed her arms and with his right hand gripped her throat; then drove his left hand, doubled into a fist, through the window glass.

Laura screamed, pushed the call button beside her bed.

Using both hands and stopping the pressure on Jimmie's throat, Clay forced her through the window. She fell heavily on the terrace. When her eyes focused after the blackness of the choking, she saw, in light from a door or window halfway between Laura's room and the corner of the building, to the right, that Clay was standing beside her with a revolver in his right hand. He was looking down, over the railing. Jimmie shouted again, hoarsely. Noises from below rose to cover the sound.

When Vicky could no longer imagine glimpses of light in the sky over the marina and had to admit that night had come, she looked toward the yellow house and saw Roberto's car still parked outside. The glazed ham, the rolls, were staying hot on the electric tray. In the absence of sherry, she had found port wine.

Six-twenty, -thirty, -forty-five. She took her bag, locked the door, and went into the square to find a taxi. But taxis rarely stopped for West Indian maids. She waited ten, fifteen minutes, then came back. The only light in the yellow house was at the kitchen level.

"I must get to the hospital," she said to Ahmad, who answered her knock. "Miss Jimmie went to be with Laura – hours ago. And taxis won't stop for me. Miss Jimmie has her car – could you use Mr. Roberto's?"

Ahmad touched her hand lightly and reassuringly with two fingers. "Of course."

"The traffic is very bad," Vicky warned as Ahmad competently and quickly started Roberto's car.

"Don't worry. I have driven in this city through upheavals before."

Victoria did not wait for Ahmad to park the car but ran past a group of nurses staring into the street at the main entrance, into the empty corridor on the first floor of the hospital, nor did she try to locate Laura's room, for she heard screaming from a higher floor. At the head of the stairs on the second floor she heard the screaming loud, desperate; followed the sound to the room from which it came on the third floor, almost stumbled over Laura, on her knees, trying to reach the doorway. Laura pointed to the window.

"Out there – outside the window."

As Vicky reached the window, Clay Austin faced her. Beyond him Vicky saw Jimmie crumpled on the terrace floor, her hands clinging to the railing.

Clay held a revolver. But the sight of the stern dark face which defied him from inside the room, a face that afflicted him like a nemesis, engulfing him in a remembered torture between fascination and repulsion – those dark faces adoring then horrified – and his own double horror – at the faces, at what he had done.

"No – no!" he cried. The hand that held the revolver twitched.

Victoria grasped the revolver and shot him twice.

Behind her Ahmad ran into the room.

Austin was slumped over the window ledge.

Still holding the revolver, Victoria, with eyes blazing, pointed an imperious hand toward the terrace.

"Bring her in."

She turned then to gather Laura into her arms and lift her into the bed. Antonio ran into the room.

"The traffic – I couldn't get here sooner." He was bending over Laura.

"She's safe," Victoria said. "Help *him*. Break out the rest of the glass."

Antonio smashed the shards and lifted Jimmie from Ahmad's arms.

At Coclé by 3:26 Diego had strung out the leads to the half-loaded truck and to the storehouse inside the wall. He worked with precision and looked almost happy. You, Roberto thought, can look happy: it's not your brother who is involved in the Condor plot, whose yacht has brought to Coclé these guns and this ammunition.

The detonator was set up under the palms where the drivers had slept. The shade there was streaked by sunlight blazing between palm fronds. Under the hard hat which he wore, his face was awash with perspiration. In the riding boots his feet felt scorched.

"How much longer?" he asked as Diego came back to the palms after checking the leads.

"Two – three minutes – and all the Condor's guts will be pulverized. And we'll be away from here."

He pumped on the detonator.

The first explosion demolished the truck, whose flaming gas tank sent blood-red gouts through the smoke and the projectiles from the ammunition. The next explosion, barely two seconds later, brought leaden fountains of ammunition from the shed, leveled the canvas-roofed house, crushed half-excavated towers and columns. In three seconds, more of the past of Coclé had been destroyed than a thousand years of foregoing time had ruined or obliterated.

In splinters of silence between eruptions Roberto thought he heard the buzzing of a helicopter but could not see it through the smoke.

Diego had started to pull in the leads from the spent charges.

"Did you hear a helicopter?" Roberto asked.

"No. My ears are too busy with the blasts. Do you still hear it?"

"No." Roberto frowned. "I wonder if it landed."

"If it had the enemy aboard, I hope it blew," Diego said.

Roberto listened for a minute or two, then as he stooped to help Diego with the leads, he heard the sound of running footsteps. He turned his head, pulled himself erect.

Three men were coming from beyond the palms.

The nearest, barely fifty feet away, squat, obese, his face dark splotched, his voice raucous, was Muñoz, shouting, with pointed revolver, "Don't move!"

Behind Muñoz, the wind blowing the black sleeves of his soutane so that he looked like a huge bat, was Father Sebastian.

A short distance apart from the other two, but nearer Muñoz, was the tall white-suited figure of Eduardo.

Obeying Muñoz's command, Roberto stood rigid. Diego, dropping the hand that had moved toward his revolver, was immobile beside him.

Eduardo did not look at his brother but at something he saw or did not see in the distance, beyond the smoking ruins from the explosions.

But Roberto looked at his brother. Now in the final death of hope that Eduardo was not a Condor, in an uncontrollable plea – for what? – in a surge of affection that

253

outweighed condemnation – he never knew what impelled him to move toward Eduardo. The motion was an involuntary summons to a revival of whatever bonds had existed between them – adoration on Roberto's part; on Eduardo's – acceptance, tolerance, a degree of affection?

Eduardo was near him now, ahead of Muñoz.

As Roberto moved, Muñoz fired.

At the movement of Muñoz's fingers on the trigger, Eduardo leaped forward. The shot from Muñoz's revolver struck him.

He fell forward, one arm extended toward Roberto.

Roberto dropped to his knees, turned Eduardo's body upward, tore open his brother's jacket, pressed a handkerchief against the gush of blood from Eduardo's chest.

Shots sounded. The sound of cars on the road – men running – Roberto did not hear above his own cries for help as he held Eduardo's body in his arms. His face was thrust against the dreadful pallor of Eduardo's when hands touched his shoulders.

"Roberto."

He tried to focus on what was outside his anguish; and looked up at Reyes's face.

"Roberto, the doctor is here. And an ambulance."

"Eduardo saved my life."

"Yes." Reyes drew him away as the doctor bent over Eduardo, then glanced at Reyes and shook his head.

Stretcher bearers came. Reyes took Roberto's arm and led him toward the road.

"Diego?" Roberto asked.

"Safe," Reyes answered. "After that first shot, he fired and struck Muñoz. Fatally."

"I will ride in the ambulance," Roberto said.

"No. You will ride with me. Here. This car. Diego will bring his truck."

Behind Reyes's car Roberto saw, in another car, beside a police guard, the black figure of the priest.

"The Father," Reyes said grimly, "has been busy trying to excommunicate my men. I don't think his threats of damnation are valid."

"How did you know – what we were doing?" Roberto asked.

"San Martín called me. With all we had to do today – well, this seemed crucial. They won't be able to do much tomorrow without the guns and the ammunition. But you – why couldn't you have reported the smuggled arms and ammunition? Why rush off to demolish them yourself?"

"Because I couldn't trust anybody in the *Guardia.*"

Reyes nodded. "Unofficially I understand. But –" he started the car – and as he did so, his radio communication unit called him. He took the message, then turned to Roberto.

"Your brother's yacht, the *Isla,* was sighted coming down – from Nicaragua? Before the Coast Guard could board, the *Isla's* crew opened the sea cocks and sank the yacht. The crew – two people – swam away. Escaped."

At least, Roberto thought, Eduardo would not need to know what happened to his loved *Isla.*

30
THE SOUTHERN CROSS

In the marina the reflections of riding lights colored pearl and silver moved with the sway of the masts. The low swell rolled against the sea wall below the upper patio where Jimmie and Roberto had sat talking for almost an hour.

From the court below the house Ahmad's

flute unscrolled soft irregular phrases.

Jimmie had come to the yellow house around midnight when she saw Roberto's lights, not knowing whether he would want to see her. On the radio she had heard what had happened at Coclé.

"Yes," he said somberly, his face unfamiliar, haggard, in the light at the doorway. "I hoped you would come."

Answering another question as they went up the broad stairway, he said, "I think a policeman brought me food – there were so many questions to answer at the station I don't remember. But I don't want anything."

"Sleep," Jimmie said. "You must have sleep."

"For both of us." He touched gently the bandage over Jimmie's left eye. "Will it be all right, *querida?*"

"It is nothing. Only a scratch on the eyelid – they took a bit of glass from my eye. And a couple of stitches."

They sat on a cushioned bench near the patio railing. Roberto's arm lay across Jimmie's shoulders. "Tell me," he said, "how you found out about Austin. Reyes gave me only pieces of the story."

Jimmie began to tell him.

They were interrupted by Ali, who came

quietly into the patio. He carried a tray with a pitcher and glasses.

"Excuse me, señor. But I have brought you lemonade. I have just heard from the radio – the chief of state has returned – rallied the loyal forces of the *Guardia*. There will be no riots tomorrow. There is no more Condor. They had no guns – ammunition – you, señor –"

"Thank you," Roberto said wearily.

"Does my brother's music disturb you, señor?"

"No," Jimmie said. "We like it."

"And so," Roberto said when Ali had left, "it was the word *whilst* that sent you to telephone Del Rio."

"Yes, that word in Uncle John's notes – Austin – his real name was Fisher – must have picked up the word in the evangelistic school he went to in Tulsa. The Del Rio police traced him there, but he had already left. The old police chief in Del Rio said he was suspected of earlier crimes. He was a killer of dark women. Before he escaped, he was being held on the charge of murdering a Negro girl. Grim thing here: the police thought the revolver he used in breaking out had been given him by a Mexican girl who'd been seen outside the back of the jail. Later the girl's body was found near there. She had been strangled. And Fisher was free. He managed to steal the card with his fingerprints."

"How he ever shed his past and wound up with a Civil Service post and enough administrative experience to get the appointment in the Canal Zone – I suppose we'll never know," Roberto said.

"And I suppose we'll never know how Uncle John recognized him after all those years. Fisher must have changed his speech habits – his appearance. But Uncle John had a penetrating mind – uncannily keen observation."

"Had Fisher met your uncle in Del Rio?"

"Yes. Uncle John had interviewed him in prison. The questions Uncle John asked at Isabel's party must have warned Fisher."

"Poor little Laura," Roberto said.

"She talked to me after – what happened. An uncomfortable man, she said. No threats – none that she could have known of – but a strangeness in his eyes. And she was frightened by something in his face when he came in and read your news sheet – the one with the notice about the snakeskin belt. Laura had left the sheet on a table. She said Fisher made her feel that he knew she had been upstairs looking for that belt. As she had."

"Thank heaven those other maids – and Antonio – interrupted Fisher, there at the fence."

"Thank heaven, indeed," Jimmie said. "She's a lovely child."

"Child – from you? She must be several years older than you, *my* child."

"Roberto, I must go back to the University. And you?"

"I will have to go. Next week."

"One more thing, Roberto. I didn't finish telling you about Tom, Isabel's stepson. Tonight while I was waiting to see you, she called and told me that two of Tom's schoolmates said Clay Austin had given out some revolvers – was training the boys to use them. Against Panamanians. Tom wouldn't talk. But these other boys objected to what was going on."

"Perhaps," Roberto said slowly, thinking, "Fisher's new personality didn't rule out some of his old repulsions from – and maybe attractions to – people he'd think of as dark."

Within the house a clock chimed twice.

"I must go back in a minute or two," Jimmie said. "Some of Vicky's family are staying with her until I come. Graci's father is going to help Vicky through the legalities." She added in a rush of

260

words, "Roberto – Victoria saved my life!"

"Eduardo saved mine," Roberto said. It was the first time he had spoken Eduardo's name since the afternoon's horror.

He withdrew his arm from Jimmie's shoulders and walked to the railing on the seaward side of the patio.

Jimmie went to stand beside him.

"Roberto, I have lived here over a year and I've never seen the Southern Cross. Not to recognize it. Can we see it from here?"

He took her hand, raised it, and pointed her fingers toward the sky.

"There," he said. "Follow a line from your first finger. You have to use imagination to make out the shape of the cross."

"Yes. I see it."

"Not a glittering constellation," Roberto said. "Pewter. Not diamonds or silver. But I've always been fond of it."

"Pewter," Jimmie said, "has substance. Endurance."

She turned from the railing, and Roberto, his hand still enclosing hers, went with her down through the house and across to the apartment building. On the second-floor landing he waited until Victoria opened the door, and then walked back to the yellow house. A guard, coming up the street from the lighted *Presidencia* waved to him as he

261

went into the house. He closed and locked the door.

In the foyer a light left burning overhead in a crystal and wrought-iron chandelier threw a frigid beam down on the breastplate of one of the two suits of armor near the door. As a child Roberto had feared the imagined presence of faceless hostile men enclosed within the steel. Now he knew them as empty monstrosities. And empty, too, was the house. Often he had come home to an empty house, but on this night the emptiness was terminal.

He walked up the broad stairway.

In his room the desk held the usual mass of papers and books. Ahmad or Ali had left his current unopened mail in a cleared space. He opened the blinds to the night, then returning to the desk, took up the letter at the top of the pile. It was from the University; and he read that he was being offered an associate professorship beginning with the next semester, and a full professorship as soon as he had completed his work for a doctorate.

A year from now? At most, a year and a half?

He took his keyring from the pocket of his jacket, slipped the larger keys away, found the small key to the middle right drawer of his desk. He unlocked the drawer and drew out the gray velvet bag that held jewels that had belonged to his mother. Among the tissue-wrapped packets he searched until he found an emerald ring in a gold setting, an ancient ring that Villalba women had worn over centuries, perhaps, he thought, from the time of Charles V.

Charles V, Philip II – he thought of the tragedy, the ferment, the overwhelming responsibilities thrust into the lives of these two men whom he believed to have been essentially simple, well-meaning; and back through the long avenues of four hundred years he acclaimed them with affection, with a relaxing of the tightness of his present grief, as if in comradeship.

Tomorrow he would give the ring to Jimmie – to Ximena – and they would chart their lives.

The publishers hope that this book has given you enjoyable reading. Large Print Books are specially designed to be as easy to see and hold as possible. If you wish a complete list of our books, please ask at your local library or write directly to: Curley Publishing, Inc., P.O. Box 37, South Yarmouth, Massachusetts, 02664.